Catbird

Catbird

A novel by

Stephen March

The Permanent Press
Sag Harbor, NY 11963

This is a work of fiction. Any resemblance to an actual person or place is coincidental.

Copyright © 2006 by Stephen March.

ISBN 1-57962-126-0 (alk. paper)

Library of Congress Cataloging-in-Publication Data

March, Stephen, 1948–
    Catbird : Stephen March.
        p.   cm.
    1. Musicians—Fiction I. Title

PS3613.A733C38 2006
813'.6—dc22   2005055342

Printed in The United States of America.

For Mary

Prologue

On certain nights when the moon was full and Lavis was on his way to getting blind drunk, he would drive Zeb out to his old homeplace on the Choctoosie River. Lavis would take Highway 11 past the Holiness Church and Wildcat Swamp where Zeb could see stars glimmering in the dark water. Past the swamp he would make a left onto the Alsace Highway, and for a time there would just be the night, the pines, and the red clay fields. Then, suddenly, he would turn off onto the gravel road leading down to the Choctoosie, the truck bouncing and rattling. Zeb could smell the river before he saw it. At the end of the road Lavis would pull off into the weeds, turn off the engine, and sit there drinking corn liquor from a Mason jar. Tree frogs and crickets would be raising hell outside, and Zeb might see the moon in the limbs of one of the oaks on the bank or hiding in a cloud above the river. The house, off to the right, was overgrown with weeds and honeysuckle. After a while, the old man would start talking, telling how his father, Elkins Dupree, a blacksmith and farmer, had moved to North Carolina from the Virginia mountains and bought the farm along the river. Elkins had married Ruth Ann Crawford, whose family lived nearby, and after her parents died Ruth inherited part of their farm, which increased the size of Elkins' land on the river. (As Lavis talked the moon might come out, allowing Zeb to see the house more clearly.)

Lavis would remember how he and his older brother Ganton used to go out on the river with their father to check the nets they had set out. They would catch herring, bass, jack, shad, catfish, and sometimes a sand shark that had swum up from the Albemarle Sound. They took the fish to the Seaton market to sell. Lavis recalled that the river often flooded the lowland, and that once or twice the water came up into the living room, giving him night-

mares about the river washing them away while they slept. He remembered ploughing with a mule, planting tobacco by hand and working with Elkins in the blacksmith shop out back: heating the metal until it was red-hot, then pounding it into shape with hammers. And he related how, after his parents died, his brother Ganton got the deed to the homeplace by paying off some back taxes Elkins had owed. Ganton promised to deed Lavis half the land, but he never did. Instead, he mortgaged the farm to finance various business ventures—a seed store, a cab company, a restaurant, all of which failed. To escape his creditors Ganton joined the Navy in 1941. He died two years later when a German sub torpedoed his ship off the coast of France. Since Lavis couldn't raise the money to pay off Ganton's mortgages, the Farmer's Bank sold the house and land at public auction. "My brother lied to me," Lavis would say bitterly. "And the only chance I ever had to own my own place went down into the cold blue sea off the coast of France. Amos Yardley owns this place now, he bought it for a fucking song, and it don't mean much more to him than a grain of sand with all the land he owns. An honest, hardworking man ain't got the chance of a pissant in hell, not in this life."

Zeb, L.C., and Merle had heard this story so often over the years they could recite it word for word. The story had become ﹋ parable about the destruction of dreams.

8

PART I

One

A man stood on the balcony, playing a saxophone, the quarter moon shining above his shoulder. His slow, sad melody drifted over the street, echoing in the courtyards and alleys below. Whistling along with the sax, Zeb Dupree walked beneath the balcony, his fiddle case under his arm. As he passed a courtyard he heard an eerie cry. The door was ajar. He pushed it open and looked around for a figure crouching in the shadows. He saw a garbage can against a far wall, a banana plant. He turned to leave, but the dismal cry came again. Removing his flask from the shoulder holster beneath his vest, he took a drink of whiskey while the saxophone rained blues notes on the street.

"Who's there?" He replaced the flask and stepped through the doorway.

The cry was coming from the garbage can.

He gave the lid a push and it clamored against the courtyard. He set the fiddle case down and plunged his hands into the refuse, feeling about until he touched something warm, alive. It was a puppy: bawling, crowned with a banana peel, sticky with coffee grounds, stinking of rotten fish. He picked up the case and carried the pup out to the sidewalk, studying it in the yellow glow of the streetlights. It was a male, a little brown ball of fur: trembling, eyes shut tight. He slipped it under his shirt and went on.

Soon he was on Royal, headed toward Canal Street. As he crossed Iberville he heard the rock and roll music and loud voices coming from Bourbon Street. If he had played there tonight he would have made more money, but he was in no mood to face the raucous crowd. He crossed Canal and went down St. Charles to the transit stop to wait for the streetcar. An old woman and a sailor stood at the transit stop. Two black girls joined them, wiggling their bodies and snapping their fingers to the music of a small radio. When the streetcar approached, everyone formed a line.

Zeb climbed the steps, dropping his coin into the money-catcher and went down the aisle past the crowded benches at the front. He took a seat next to an old man with a white goatee and a black string tie. The streetcar was brightly illuminated by a string of bare bulbs around the top. A black curtain separated the conductor from the passengers.

As the streetcar rattled up St. Charles, Zeb unbuttoned his shirt and pulled the puppy's head out so it could breathe. The old man man sitting next to Zeb gave him a sharp, disgusted look.

"Got a pup here," Zeb said. "Someone threw him out."

The man frowned and looked out the window.

The streetcar stopped again, and an old black man got on, singing in a loud, drunken voice. He wore a T-shirt, golf cap, and baggy trousers supported by purple suspenders. Clutching a leather strap that hung from the bar overhead, he looked around as if perplexed. His gaze fell on two nuns sitting in front row seats to his right. Their black-shawled heads were sleek as bowling balls beneath the hot lights.

"Murderers!" he cried, aiming his finger at the nuns. "Dealers in death and misery!"

"That nigger is crazy," said the man sitting next to Zeb.

"Cursed are those who pollute the lives of children!"

"Go to hell!" someone cried from the back of the streetcar.

"Ladies and gentlemen," the old man said, "they ain't real sisters. I know these women. They're imposters."

One of the nuns said something sharp and hateful-sounding to their accuser.

"You can't fool me," he shouted, shaking his fist. "You snake-eyed hussies!"

The streetcar came to a sudden stop, throwing the old man to the floor. Two men rushed down the aisle, seized him, and began dragging him toward the front. A woman struck him with her purse. A man kicked him. The conductor opened the door and the men dragged him, shouting and complaining, down the steps and over the pavement to the sidewalk.

"There's nothing sacred any more!" he cried.

The men got back on and the streetcar started to roll. The old man was a forlorn heap on the sidewalk.

He was asking for trouble, Zeb thought. Trying to start a fight with the sisters. Still, he couldn't help feeling sorry for the man.

The man with the goatee got off at the next stop, and Zeb moved over to take the seat by the window. A copper-colored girl in a green dress sat down beside him. They were now in the Garden District, passing huge old homes bejeweled with lights. Zeb took the puppy from under his shirt. One eye was swollen shut, the other full of mucus.

The girl touched the pup's nose. "He stinks."

"I found him in a trash can."

"I believe it."

The pup whined, trembled, licked his fingers.

Zeb got off at Loyola University and walked in the direction of his apartment, three blocks away. He lived in a three-room flat on the second floor of a white frame house.

When he came to the house, he climbed the stairway at the back and went inside, immediately inspecting the kitchen for signs of a conjugal visit: a note, lipstick on a coffee cup, something missing. But the place looked the same as when he left: beer cans on the table, the sink full of dirty dishes. He put the puppy down, but it only lay on its belly and whimpered. He set a bowl of milk in front of it. The pup kept whining. He pushed its face into the bowl. The pup licked its chin, then began lapping the milk.

He sat down at the table and took a drink from the flask.

He had not seen his wife in three days and nights, and without her there the place was like a tomb.

He woke up the next morning and sat on the side of the bed, his head throbbing like a mashed thumb. He had been dreaming about Lavis. In the dream Lavis was sitting at his workbench in the barn. He was wearing a navy, pinstriped suit, his shoes were shined, and his hair slicked down. It was an odd dream since Zeb could count on one hand the number of times he had seen his father in a suit.

Groaning, he got up and went down the hall to the john. His urine was bright yellow, full of poisons. An empty tampon box on

12

the back of the toilet reminded him that his wife had been gone for four days.

He went through the living room to the kitchen where he stepped in something wet—puppy piss. He got a beer from the refrigerator and sat at the table. He remembered discussing a separation agreement with his wife—how long ago had it been, five days, a week? She'd had a list of their property: the shares in the mutual fund, the savings account containing the profit and equity derived from the sale of their home, the new Buick, the furniture, most of it in storage. They agreed she was to receive everything except one fourth of the savings. It wasn't the settlement that bothered Zeb—he was past caring about their common possessions—but her cool, businesslike manner during the discussion.

The puppy was trembling against his foot. Zeb took him into the bathroom and cleaned the open eye with cotton and boric acid. The other eye was a mass of red and purple. Evidently something, or someone, had gouged it out. He bathed the pup in the tub, dried him off with a towel, and fed him some milk and cereal. Then he mopped the kitchen floor.

He spent the rest of the morning packing his clothes and books into cardboard boxes and carrying them out to his truck, a gunmetal blue 1964 Dodge with 130,000 miles on the odometer. He had bought it from a Cajun two days earlier, since Roseanne got the Buick. During one trip the retired fireman who lived downstairs came out to water his azaleas. His wife peeped out from behind a curtain in the window. Zeb guessed she had sent him out to find out what was going on. They knew his wife was gone.

The fireman had paid them a visit the day they moved in, to find out if Zeb liked to bowl and what kind of work he did—a painful subject for him since he had only recently been fired as editor of *The Bayou Journal,* a newspaper covering suburban New Orleans. Zeb told the man he was looking for a job playing in a band. His neighbor said he didn't know much about music: all he knew about was fire fighting and bowling. He was captain of his bowling team, and during his thirty-three years as a Louisiana fireman he had put out every kind of fire there was. Observing that the man seemed immensely proud of his life, Zeb had felt both amazement and envy.

On his way back from the truck he passed his neighbor watering his azaleas. "Where's your wife?" the man asked.

13

"Gone."

"With that other feller?"

"That's right."

The man shook his head, as if confounded by a mystery too profound for a mortal mind to grasp. "Folks don't stay together anymore. Look at the mess the government is in. The morals of this country have been going to the dogs ever since that rock and roll music hit back in the fifties. All that tutti-frutti stuff."

Zeb went up the stairs, pondering the dubious connection between Little Richard and Big Richard, the nation's former leader who had resigned in disgrace. Jack Griming, Zeb's boss at *The Bayou Journal,* had claimed that history would vindicate Nixon as "one of America's greatest leaders." But Zeb wasn't sure. He thought he had observed a certain look in the president's eyes which Lavis used to call "an egg-sucking look." Lavis said a dog with an egg-sucking look could never be trusted.

Along with the boxes of books and clothes, Zeb packed in the truck bed a mattress, a rocking chair, a card table, his typewriter, some sheets and blankets, kitchen utensils, and his shotgun. Then he went back upstairs, sat down at the table, and composed a letter:

> *I'll be in Cedar Springs if you want to get in touch. Write me in care of general delivery.*
> *I'll be missing you.*
> *Zeb*

Leaving the note on the table, he gathered up his fiddle, his wallet, and the pills he had acquired from various dealers in the Quarter. He put the black beauties in his vest pocket, his fiddle under his arm, and, lighting a cigar, he picked up the pup and went down to his truck. He put the pup in a box on the seat and drove off without looking back.

Above the city, on the expressway, he looked down at the buildings, gray-blue in the hazy light and tipped with clouds, the sky the dull silver color of a dead trout. He turned on the radio, flipped cigar ashes out the window, and beat his fingers against the steering wheel in time to the Cajun music. The music was followed by the morning news. An item in the broadcast caught his attention:

14

". . . members of the New Orleans Vice Squad arrested the two women late last night following an anonymous tip. The women, who were disguised as nuns, had a large quantity of cocaine in their possession."

The nuns on the streetcar. Come to think of it, there *had* been something strange about them—the way they were so hateful to the old man. Had he tipped off the vice squad?

Soon Zeb was on the bridge spanning Lake Ponchartrain, the water below a darker shade of silver than the sky. The sun was a hot pink disc on the horizon. He washed down a black beauty with a swallow of warm beer. He was heading toward Cedar Springs, North Carolina. It was close enough to his hometown that he could visit Jadine, L.C., and Merle without having them observe his every move. Also, many fine string bands had flourished in Cedar Springs back when he had been a student at Cedar Springs State University. He hoped he could find a job playing his fiddle.

He hit Tuscaloosa, Alabama at twilight and took another black beauty. The hours were gliding by like sailboats. He was moving so fast he had already outrun his pain. He could feel it back there in the night, hurrying to catch up.

At noon the next day Zeb parked his truck on Jefferson Street, in front of Cedar Springs State. He had been driving all night. Resting his forehead against the steering wheel, he could feel himself tumbling into a dark lagoon. He was jolted awake by an incessant jingling and chanting. He stared at the ivy-covered administration building where the Beaumont Scholarship Committee had interviewed him his senior year in high school. Several students sat on the stone wall that ran along the edge of the sidewalk. Behind, on the grass, a group of Hare Krishnas danced, chanted, pounded on drums.

He got out of the truck, carried the pup over to the grass. After it urinated, he put it back in the truck and crossed the street to a cafe, where he ordered ham and eggs. Halfway through his meal, he remembered coming to this same cafe with his wife. He pictured her coming to the apartment and finding his note. She would be with her lover. He pushed the plate away and went to the counter to pay his bill.

15

Outside, a young man in a cowboy hat stood on the sidewalk, strumming a guitar and singing. Zeb dropped a quarter into his opened guitar case and went on, passing a bar, a clothing store, and a shop with bong pipes, T-shirts, and university pennants hanging in the windows. Ahead, on the sidewalk, sat a black woman surrounded by cans full of red and yellow flowers. A flower vendor. Across the street was the old Cosmic City Dance Hall. A neon sign hung over the front of the building: an image of a cat being struck by a bolt of lightning. A sign below read, *The Electric Cat.* He crossed the street and walked back to his truck. He had to find a place to sleep. After considering the truck, he remembered a building several blocks north on Jefferson Street where rooms could be rented by the week. Only the poorest students had lived in the building, which residents called "the Tombs," along with an assortment of dishwashers, winos, and others down on their luck. The first floor of the building housed a drug store and flower shop. The manager of the flower shop had also managed the Tombs.

Zeb found the manager at the back of the shop, trimming roses. A beefy man with a German accent, he said he didn't usually have rooms available on such short notice; however, due to "an unfortunate incident" a room had become available only yesterday. The manager took Zeb outside and up the stairs next door to show him the room, which smelled of disinfectant and fish. The previous tenant had been "a weirdo," the manager explained, who stayed in his room all day and ate only canned sardines and peanut butter. Three days earlier the man had dragged his mattress into the bathroom down the hall and set it afire, claiming it was haunted by evil spirits. "This is a quiet place," the manager added. "We don't like freaks."

"How much is the room?"

"Twenty-five dollars a week, plus twenty dollars security deposit, payable in advance. No loud music, no pets. Take it or leave it."

After paying for the room Zeb drove the truck around to the parking lot in back and began carrying his possessions up the fire escape. He took the mattress up last, on his back, the pup hidden under his shirt.

In the bathroom down the hall from his room he was mugged by some vicious odors—urine, bleach, Lysol, burnt mattress. A black spot on the concrete floor leaped out like a huge psychiatric ink blot, daring him to reveal the demoniac figures writhing inside. He checked the wall for interesting graffiti but found only racial slurs, vulgar ditties, telephone numbers, and solicitations for gay sex. On the wall over one of the urinals he read,

We have escaped from the mattress
and are living in the walls.

The Evil Spirits.

He returned to his room and fed the puppy the biscuit he had slipped into his pocket at the restaurant. He gave it water in a Dixie cup. Then he took a Valium and stretched out on the bed. He could still see Jefferson Street in his mind, but the singer, students, flower lady, and Hare Krishnas were floating in the air. Books, flowers, drums, and a guitar floated around, too, parking meters glowed like neon, and in the sky where the sun should have been, there was the flashing neon sign of the electric cat.

The pup woke him up licking his ear.

He cleaned up the mess in the corner with paper towels from the bathroom. Then he put the pup under his shirt and went down the hall to the fire escape. Stepping out onto the metal landing he saw the pink neon hog floating in the night sky above Whitmore Street, which ran parallel to Jefferson. The hog hovered above a restaurant that specialized in barbecue. Zeb envisioned a plate of barbecue served with slaw, potato salad, and hush puppies, but the foul smell arising from the dumpsters below quickly sabotaged his hunger. He went down the steps and set the pup on the pavement.

"This is where you do your business," he said. "Not inside. Go ahead now."

But the pup only huddled against his foot, whining.

He took the pup back up to the room. There he stripped and sat down on one of the boxes, staring at his withered leg in the glare of the bulb hanging from the ceiling. He felt all of the old shame and disgust. On his honeymoon in Key West, he and Roseanne had been walking on the beach, and they'd heard a child cry, "Mama, look at that man's leg! What's wrong with his leg?"

Floorboards creaking in the hallway brought back an old memory. Asleep in his bedroom, Zeb had been awakened by the sound of the stairs creaking. Lavis had come into the room and shaken his shoulder. "Time to watch the 'bacca, boy." Zeb sat up, listening to his father descend the stairs. The pungent aroma of curing tobacco lingered in the room. Lavis had been at the curing barn since early afternoon, tending the fire. Zeb picked up the flashlight and went down the stairs, barefoot. Outside, the cornstalks gossiped in the wind as he walked down the winding road to the curing barn. The air was drenched with the rich tobacco smell. He opened the door, shined the flashlight at the thermometer on the wall. It was 140 degrees. Tobacco needed to cure at 148 degrees. He pushed a log into the flue and sat on the ground, firing a tobacco stick rifle at marauding Indians. He could hear the wind in the maples. He lay on his back on the ground, counting the stars. The stars are pieces of silver in a pirate's chest, he thought. When the old bastard falls asleep, I'll steal them.

He woke up with Lavis shaking him. He was afraid his father would be angry at him for falling asleep while entrusted with the care of the tobacco, but Lavis only picked him up and carried him toward the house. Zeb could see his father's jaw line angled against the stars. In one ear he could hear Lavis' beating heart; in the other, the wind voices murmuring in the corn.

The puppy woke him up again, whining. A roach scurried along the floor, carefully avoiding a seam of sunlight. Zeb covered his eyes with his arm. He could see Jadine sitting at her kitchen table, her Bible in her hands. He knew he should call her, but then he would have to answer questions he didn't want to have to think about. He put more boric acid into the puppy's eyes. The swelling was going down in the blind eye. The other one appeared to be clearing up, too. He fed the pup a candy bar and some crackers. After a visit to the john, he went down the stairs to the sidewalk.

The sun hurt his eyes as he walked. He went into a bar and grill and ordered a bowl of chili and a beer. Then he went back to the john to wash his hands. On the wall over the sink, he read:

You are standing in the Devil's shadow.

His spine tingling, he returned to the counter where he swallowed a Valium with his beer. He was going to have to get his act together. He was going to have to rebuild his life, one day at a time. The first step was to find a job playing in a band.

He caught the attention of the man behind the counter.

"Do you know of any bands around here that need a fiddler?"

"Ask in the Saloon, on up Jefferson."

After Zeb left the bar and grill he walked on up Jefferson Street toward the Saloon, four blocks north of the Tombs. Formerly Cedar Springs' old Southern Railway station, the Saloon had been converted into a bar and dance hall back when he was a student at Cedar Springs State. As he climbed the steps to the wooden deck in front of the Saloon, he noticed a poster on the front door, an advertisement for an upcoming performance by a band, Little Brown Jug. The heavy wooden door opened onto a breezeway. To the right there was a room with pool tables. The old waiting room was to the left, a long, spacious room with a beamed ceiling and hardwood floor. Some tables and chairs faced a platform at the far end of the room, where the bands played.

He ordered a beer at the bar and asked the bartender about the band on the poster.

"Little Brown Jug is about the best acoustic band around here," the bartender said.

"I've been gone from Cedar Springs a few years. Where are the good places to hear acoustic music?"

"This is it. Cedar Springs is a rock and roll town now."

"You know of any bands that might need a fiddler?"

"Duane might know." The bartender nodded at the Saloon's only other customer, a lanky young man in paint-spattered overalls.

"There's only a few country or old-time bands around here," Duane said. "As far as I know, they've all got fiddlers."

"Duane, you used to be in a band, didn't you?" the bartender asked.

"Yeah, but that's history now, Sloe Gin."

"Why'd you give it up?"

"I spent two years living from one gig to the next, always dreaming of hitting the big time. Woke up one morning in a motel room in Amarillo, Texas with something cold against the back of my neck. It was my girlfriend's arm. She'd mixed a handful of pills with a fifth of Mexican tequila, and she was like a slab of ice." Duane took a swallow of beer from his mug, wiped his mouth with the back of his hand. "Not long after that I developed a passionate new interest in painting houses."

Zeb studied his palm, recalling his visit to Madam Lavette, a palm reader well-known in the Quarter for her accurate prophesies.

"You have a broken fate line," Madam Lavette had said. "This suggests a life with many peaks and valleys. I see a deep valley just ahead."

"What about the peaks? Do you see any peaks?"

"I see a dark cloud falling, trouble in the heart. Treachery from someone close to you."

A week later, he'd found out about his wife's lover.

The day after his conversation with Sloe Gin and Duane in the Saloon, Zeb got a job washing dishes at Lorenzo's, a Mexican restaurant near the university. He worked from five PM until one AM, busing tables and washing dishes. His co-workers were H. T. Slocum, a black man in his late twenties, and Uriah Bozely, an old vagabond who lived at the Tombs. Uriah claimed to know every plate in the kitchen by its name. "This is Eric," he would say, touching a plate, "and this gentleman here is Mr. Thomas. This is Mabeline, this is Ruby and this is Miss Jessica." He was as proud of each plate as if it had been an orchid he had raised. At first Zeb was skeptical about Uriah's claim; he would hide plates the old man had named and show them to him later. Uriah always named the dishes correctly.

Busing tables and washing dishes was hard on Zeb's crippled leg. The work put so much pressure on his bad knee that it stayed swollen and tender. Whenever he became too depressed about his job, he would laugh at it, which helped relieve his misery. Once, during a busy night, Lorenzo, the owner, came into the kitchen and caught him laughing on the job. "Why are you laughing?" Lorenzo demanded. Zeb shrugged, and kept on laughing.

"Keep your mind on your job, Dupree!"

Lorenzo, a tall, brooding man, seemed like someone who would be in charge of cadavers rather than tortillas. Zeb had heard H.T. say that Lorenzo opened the restaurant with his mother's money.

At night when Zeb got off work, he would return to his room and clean up any mess the puppy had made. Then he would take the pup out to the alley and sit on the landing of the fire escape, smoking a cigar to kill the smell of the dumpsters. Some nights Uriah would join him on the fire escape, and they would share a bottle of wine.

"You ought to give that pup a name," Uriah told him one night. "How would you feel if you had to go through life without a name?"

"Thought about calling him 'Trouble.'"

"You give him a name like that, he's liable to live up to it."

After meditating on the pup awhile, Uriah said he thought it looked like a "Henry," so that's what Zeb started calling him. Uriah was convinced Henry was mostly bluetick with some beagle and shepherd thrown in, but Zeb believed he was more of a walker with a dash or two of bluetick and a sprinkle of black lab. When he told Uriah how he had found Henry, the old man said that anyone who would throw a sick, half-blind pup into a garbage can ought not to have anything to eat except hot chili peppers.

Except for Uriah, Zeb didn't talk much to the building's other residents. They came in late at night carrying wine bottles in paper bags. Sometimes he heard them mumbling to themselves as they passed by.

The high point of Zeb's first month in Cedar Springs came the night he listened to Little Brown Jug in the Saloon. It was a five-piece old-time band—fiddle, bass, mandolin, guitar, and banjo—with some of the sweetest harmonies he had ever heard. Little Brown Jug played many of his old favorites, like "Arkansas Traveler," plus a selection of Irish and bluegrass tunes. Zeb sat at the bar, swilling beer, clapping his hands and stomping his feet. "Hot damn!" he cried. "Tear it up!" Music like that made a man feel like he had a chance in the world.

Next morning he went down to the Cedar Springs Post Office to see if Roseanne had written him.

"Nothing for you today," The clerk said.

Zeb called his mother, Jadine, one night from the pay phone on the sidewalk in front of the Tombs.

"Hey, Mama. It's me."

"Zeb! Where are you?"

"Cedar Springs."

"I've been worried sick. Why haven't you called?"

"I'm sorry. I've had a lot on my mind."

"I tried to call you in New Orleans, and I got a recording, saying the phone had been disconnected. I called Mrs. Lamar and she said you and Roseanne had separated."

"A lot's happened, Mama."

"I should say so. Why'd you and Roseanne split up?"

"I don't want to talk about it now. I'll explain everything when I come home."

"When will that be?"

"Day after tomorrow."

"Promise?"

"Yes. I'll be there around noon."

After he hung up Zeb went up to his room and got out his fiddle. His chest hurt, and he had a sour taste in his mouth. He took his fiddle out to the fire escape and began working on a new jazz tune he was trying to master. His fiddle always challenged him to go beyond the existing limits of his skill. The instrument would meet him in a place that transcended space and time. It was the one thing that had always been equal to his love.

Two

The summer Zeb turned twelve he and L.C. stole a tennis racket, a single-shot .22 rifle, and a fiddle out of the widow Welch's barn. L.C. laid claim to the .22 since the larceny had been his idea. They threw the tennis racket away, so Zeb's share of the loot was the fiddle. He kept it hidden under his bed, thinking he would trade it for a shotgun to Oscar Deloatch, fiddler for the Swamp Foxes, the county's most popular string band. But Jadine found the fiddle and demanded to know where it had come from. She didn't believe his story, that he had found it in a ditch, and he'd had to get L.C. to corroborate his claim.

Oscar, a big, red-faced farmer with a handlebar mustache, lived on his farm a mile away, toward Seaton. One sweltering August afternoon Zeb walked down to his house, toting the fiddle. He found Oscar sitting on his front porch swing, fanning himself with a copy of *The Seaton Gazette.*

"Say, Oscar, sure is hot, ain't it."

"Right warm. What you got there?"

Zeb opened the case and put it on Oscar's lap.

"What you doing with Grady Welch's old fiddle?"

"Ain't his. Me and L.C. found it in a ditch."

Oscar tightened and resined the bow, and, clasping the fiddle beneath his chin, he tuned it. Then he began playing. His body swayed, the bow moved magically over the strings, his fingers flew over the fingerboard. Zeb's mouth dropped open in amazement, for Oscar was creating the most beautiful music he had ever heard.

"You ought to learn to play it," Oscar said, returning the fiddle and bow to the case.

Zeb plucked a string. "I was figuring on trading it for a shotgun before dove season comes in."

Oscar's eyebrows shot up, and for a terrifying moment he resembled old Grady Welch, who had committed suicide by diving into his well.

"I'm ass-deep in fiddles." He closed the case and handed it to Zeb. "Fiddle's got a sweet tone. Sounded better when Grady had it, but then he ain't been playing it much lately."

Oscar began whistling one of the tunes he had been playing. The melody followed Zeb down the road.

Back home, he sat on his bed, drawing the bow across the strings. It made a shrill, scratching sound. He continued playing, his eyes closed, pretending he was playing as good as Oscar. When he opened his eyes, he was staring into the black bore of L.C.'s .22 inches from his face.

"We came to put whatever was dying out of its misery," L.C. said. Merle stood behind him, both of them snickering.

"You'd better point that gun somewhere else," Zeb said, "if you don't want to eat it."

Next day, he went back to see Oscar.

"Can you teach me to play it?"

Oscar looked out at his cornfield. "Fiddle's a hard thing to learn."

"I'd like to try."

"I can teach you, but I'll have to charge you."

"How much?"

"Fifty cents a lesson. That might sound high, but I want you to take it serious."

Zeb got the money from Jadine by agreeing to sweep the kitchen and back porch every day and wash the dishes on Saturday night so she could watch *Gunsmoke*. She took the money out of the grocery budget.

Oscar taught him how to hold the fiddle and bow properly and how to draw the bow across the strings smoothly, keeping his wrist and arm relaxed. The bow felt awkward at first, like a saw, and the scales Oscar kept insisting he play put Zeb in mind of the shotgun he might have been able to get in exchange for the fiddle. But he kept at it. Oscar finally taught him his first tune, "Bile Them Cabbage Down." Zeb played the tune all the way home. He played it in the kitchen, bedroom, and den, and he was playing it on the back porch when Jadine sent him down to the barn.

He continued taking lessons from Oscar. By winter, he had learned a dozen tunes, and he was trying to master more advanced techniques like shuffles, double notes, drones and slurs. At night he would listen to the Grand Ole Opry on the radio, to songs by Bill Monroe and the Bluegrass Boys, the Stanley Brothers and the Blue Sky Boys, who sang such wistful tunes as "When I Take My Vacation in Heaven" and "Don't This Road Look Rough and Rocky?" Zeb would get out his fiddle and play along.

That spring Rainy Bowden, who owned the farm they lived on, began sending Lavis in to fetch him out to play for him while he sat in his truck drinking whiskey. Zeb would play songs like "Flop-Eared Mule" and "Cotton-Eyed Joe."

"Hot damn," Rainy would cry. "Tear it up!"

Lavis would buck dance in the yard, and sometimes the old rooster in the peach tree would wake up and crow.

Three

An hour east of Cedar Springs, Zeb left the rolling hill country of
the Piedmont for the flat red fields of the Coastal Plain. He passed
tin-roofed shanties, swamps filled with black water and cypress,
white frame churches, farmhouses, and abandoned country stores
swarming with kudzu. He was in a country of trucks, juke joints,
and billboards that advertised everything from Red Man tobacco
to Kill-Em-Dead pesticide. "Life will be beautiful if you look at
it through the eyes of faith," said a voice on the radio. "Reach out
to God's unchanging hand. He'll heal the broken-hearted and
redeem the souls of his faithful servants. He is the great deliverer;
he is the man called Jesus." Zeb turned the dial, looking for a
country music station.

He drove into Seaton on 48 East, passing the new consolidated
Seaton High School on the left. The country had built the new
school two years after Zeb graduated from high school—after the
federal government forced the county board to abolish its separate
systems based on race. He turned right at the stoplight onto
Highway 11 and drove past the old Seaton High School on the
right; it was a junior high now. Since most of the county's white
students now attended private schools, the public schools were
predominantly black.

The farm was four miles south of the town limits, a mile past
the poultry processing plant where Jadine and Merle worked.
As Zeb turned into the driveway, the farmhouse glowed in the
hazy noon light, like mother-of-pearl. He parked in the yard
behind the house and stared at Lavis' battered '60 Ford pickup
parked in front of the barn. The windshield was cracked, and two
tires were flat.

Jadine came out the back door of the farmhouse and stood on the sagging porch. She wore a frayed sweater over a cotton dress. Zeb could tell by the way her mouth was set that she was going to give him hell.

"Where'd you get the puppy?"

"He followed me home," he said, kissing her on the cheek.

"What's wrong with his eye?"

"He got it put out."

"Come on in, but leave him outside."

Zeb set the puppy down and followed his mother into the kitchen. Her black-bound Bible was open on the table.

"You hungry?"

"Yes, ma'am."

"I have to heat up the peas and grits." Jadine went to the stove and turned on the burners beneath two pots. The sausage she had fried earlier was on a paper plate on the counter.

Zeb sat down at the table and stared at the faded print of *The Last Supper* on the wall. Next to the print was a photo of L.C. in his Army fatigues, holding up a big green lizard he had shot in Vietnam. L.C., who held the lizard by its tail, was smiling proudly in the photo, as if he were holding a record-breaking bass.

Jadine sat down in the chair next to him. "You had a wife, a job, and a home, and now they're gone. What happened?"

"Everything just fell apart."

"You can do better than that."

"She wanted kids, Mama. Seems we couldn't have any."

"Did you see a doctor?"

"Yes ma'am. Everything was O.K. We just couldn't get a hit."

"What was the name of the minister at your church?" Jadine had met him when she visited one Easter.

"Reverend Wright."

"Did you talk to him?"

"He was deaf."

"Deaf?"

"That's right. He was supposed to be able to read lips, but that was a crock."

Jadine's eyes had turned dark gray, the color they got when she was angry.

"Mrs. Lamar said you got fired from the newspaper. Is that true?"

"Yes, ma'am."

"Why didn't you tell me?"

"Didn't want to worry you."

"So you let me hear about it from her?"

"She thinks it's my fault, doesn't she?"

"What do you think?"

"I don't know, Mama. I'm all mixed up."

"I tried to do right by you, son. Now didn't I try to do right by you?"

"Yes, ma'am."

"I took you to church. I taught you about the Lord. I've prayed for you. I've laid awake nights worrying myself sick about you. What else can I do?"

"I've just had a run of bad luck lately, Mama. It's nothing permanent."

"When did you get fired?"

"It's a long story, but I'm glad it happened."

"You're glad you got fired?"

"I was tired of newspaper work."

His mother stared at him, shaking her head.

"I was so proud of you when you went off to college. You got an education and a decent job, and now you've just thrown it away—for what?"

Zeb looked down at his hands. He had a dull throbbing in the back of his head.

Jadine got up and went to the stove. She spooned out grits, peas, and sausage onto a plate, then set the plate on the table in front of him, along with a glass of iced tea. "There's biscuits in the oven. They'll be ready soon."

Although he had no appetite, he took a bite of food.

"Aren't you going to say grace first?"

He bowed his head, trying to think of some words of prayer, but his effort was interrupted by a disturbing image—the Reverend Lamar, Roseanne's father, glaring at him. He counted to ten, then resumed eating. "How's L.C. and Merle?"

"L.C. is still at the Gulf Station. He's driving the wrecker now, working a lot of nights so I don't see him much. Merle is doing real well. Mr. Hines, the plant manager, has taken a shine to him. Last month he took Merle off the line and made him an inspector. He got a fifty-cents-an-hour raise."

Merle had been working at Finley's Processing about a year. Jadine had been there six months; she'd had to start working after Lavis died.

"How do you like your job, Mama?"

"What's to like about it? I stand at a conveyor belt all day. The chickens roll by, plucked and scalded. I slice them open, take out the organs, and throw them into a trough, except for the heart, liver, and gizzard. I stick them back into the chicken."

Zeb put down his fork and rubbed his temples. The pain in the back of his head had spread to the front.

"What's Roseanne doing in New Orleans?"

"She's shacking up with a guy if you want to know the truth."

"What?"

"She's giving him everything she used to give me."

"And her a minister's daughter."

Henry was whining and yelping outside. Zeb pushed back his chair and stood up. "I'm going to check on the pup."

Outside, he bent over Henry, scratching his head, then he walked down to the pickup by the barn. He stared through the cracked windshield at the truck's interior and remembered the last time he had seen Lavis. Zeb and Roseanne had been visiting Seaton from New Orleans, and he had stopped by the farm to tell his parents goodbye. He had found Lavis at his workbench in the barn, tinkering with a carburetor. A light fastened to the wall shown on his scarred, blunt-fingered hands. "We're heading back, Daddy," Zeb said. The old man's eyes were red, unfocused; his breath reeked of last night's whiskey. He mumbled something about having a safe trip.

I should have offered him my hand, Zeb thought.

The barn was leaning to the left, a brown, mottled parallelogram. Every year the angle got sharper. He stepped inside and immediately felt a sharp pain in his chest. The sour, damp smell choked him. He backed out quickly and crossed the yard to the dirt road that ran back to the tobacco barn, the pup at his heels. The brown, withered cornstalks rattled in the wind. Daddy spent more than twenty years of his life working this land, Zeb thought bitterly, and now there's nothing to show for his labor except that broken plough point in the ditch.

He went on to the log tobacco barn. Inside, he pictured Eula Hogan straddling a top tier as she tied up the tobacco leaves. Eula, a black girl who helped them out at harvest time, had become the object of L.C. and Zeb's desire the summer her breasts began to swell. Zeb remembered the time L.C. exposed himself to her behind the tobacco barn. "Come on, Eula, touch it," he pleaded, while Zeb and Merle watched from a clump of honeysuckle. "Get away from me, L. C," Eula cried. "You nasty thing!"

Zeb walked on down the road, back through the pines to the abandoned hog lot. The feeder was turned over, its bottom rusting out. He remembered how Lavis used to take a sack of corn out to the hogs in the evening. He would lean over the fence and scratch their backs while they ate.

I wish I'd shook his hand, he thought.

Walking back to the house, he saw L.C.'s red Chevy pickup parked in the yard. L.C. and Merle were waiting for him on the porch. They came down the steps and exchanged bear hugs with him in the yard.

"Where'd you get that pitiful mutt?" L.C. asked.

"Found him in a trash can."

"I believe it." L.C. put an arm around Zeb's shoulders. "I'm glad you're here, Zeb. You've arrived in the nick of time. Baby brother here is fixing to get himself in trouble. His favorite wench wants him to settle down and make babies before he's had the chance to experience the full range of pleasures life has to offer him."

"Is that true, Merle?"

"L.C.'s ass is sucking canal water. Besides, he's screwing so many different girls he gets their names mixed up in the dark."

"Now that's a fact. Other night I called Diane 'Margot.' Made her so mad she'd liked to have shit a little gold monkey."

Jadine opened the screen door.

"Zeb, aren't you going to eat?"

"I'm coming."

"L.C., Merle—you boys want a bite to eat?"

They went into the house and sat at the table. Jadine served L.C. and Merle the grits, peas, and sausage, along with hot biscuits.

"Who's the stranger, Mama?" L.C. asked, nodding at Zeb.

"That's your brother, Zeb. I'd just about forgotten what he looks like, too."

"I believe he's gotten uglier," Merle said.

"Impossible," said L.C.

"I wish you'd come to church with me tomorrow, Zeb," Jadine said. "I want you to hear our new preacher, Reverend Beasley. All the young people in our church are crazy about him, aren't they, L.C.?"

"Yes, ma'am, they sure are," L.C. said, giving Zeb a wink.

Just before dusk Zeb, Merle, and L. C went for a ride in L.C.'s truck. They stopped at a 7-Eleven and filled up the cooler in the back of the truck with beer and ice; then they headed out to the Alsace Highway drinking beer, listening to a George Jones tape. After a while, Merle asked Zeb what had happened between him and Roseanne.

"She found somebody she liked better," he said.

"Who was it?"

"Guy she met in a class she was taking." Zeb looked out the window. The sky was orange and lavender above the fields. "I wanted to kill the son of a bitch, but there wasn't anything I could do except let her go."

L.C. accelerated, passing a truck hauling a load of hogs. "You need to go out with some other women and put Roseanne out of your mind."

"That's right," said Merle. "You need to get some honey on your stinger."

"Yessiree Bob," L.C. said, as he popped the top on a beer. "Ain't nothing like a little pussy to ease a broken heart."

The sun had gone down and the moon had come out when L.C. turned down the dirt road leading to the Choctoosie River. Zeb could see the river ahead, luminous in the moonlight, the oaks on the bank hung with Spanish moss. L.C. parked in the weeds, and they got out and walked toward the house. The moon was big and gold, with red veins.

"This looks snaky," Merle said, wading through the weeds.

"Fuck a damned snake," L.C. said.

The boards creaked as they went up the steps. The front door was gone. Merle shined a flashlight inside. Something flew by, and they all flinched.

"Ain't nothing but a little old bat," Zeb said.

They went into the living room, L.C. kicking boards out of the way. The house smelled dank, musty. Merle's light moved around in the darkness, revealing beams, bottles, trash. Part of the second floor had caved in. Stars glimmered through a hole in the roof.

"Reckon there's ghosts in here?" Merle asked.

"Hell, yes, there's ghosts," L.C. said. "Where do you think ghosts hang out, in a skating rink?"

There was a shrill, moaning sound upstairs.

"What the hell?" Merle pointed the light up at the broken beams.

"The wind," Zeb said.

"It's liable to be Grandpa," L.C. said.

"I'm getting out of here," Merle said.

Zeb and L.C. followed him outside, down the steps into the weeds. There was a rattling sound on the roof.

"Piece of tin blowing," Zeb said.

They went back to the truck and sat there sipping beer, looking out at the river. L.C. lit a joint and passed it around.

"I still can't figure why Daddy did it," Merle said, after a while.

"I don't understand why he did it that way," L.C. said. "Where she'd find him."

"Last time I saw him he was talking about rats being in his truck," Merle said.

"The rats were in his fucking head," Zeb said.

They were quiet awhile, then L.C. began talking in a low, hypnotic voice.

"Back in 'Nam we were searching this village the V.C. had been using as a storage base. We lined the old chief and his family up in front of a ditch, and the captain started asking them questions. I'd been smoking hash all morning, and the gooks seemed weird, unreal. They had their hands up in the air, and they kept jabbering, shaking their heads. The captain's voice got louder and madder. Then he stepped back and gave the order to fire. I couldn't believe it. I heard the M-16s going off. I just stood there, watching those people falling back into the ditch. Then the captain was

32

shouting "Fire, fire!" in my ear. I pointed my rifle at the ground, closed my eyes, and pulled the trigger. I kept pulling it, not knowing if I hit anyone or not. I wasn't aiming at them, just shooting in the ground. When I looked again they were all down in the ditch. Men, women, children, old people. Shot all to hell.

"I got crazy after that. I'd just lay around stoned, not eating. I kept seeing those gooks. I'd even dream about them. Sometimes I was killing them, other times I'd be laying in the ditch with them. I still see those people. I can see them right now."

L.C. started up the engine and backed the truck out of the weeds. He gunned the engine on the dirt road and hit the highway doing 70.

L.C., Merle, and Zeb sat at a table in the corner of Lou's Diner in Seaton, watching the waitress behind the counter.

"Poetry in motion," said Merle.

"She looks even better without the uniform," L.C. said. "Hey, Maxine, how about some service?"

"Keep your pants on, L.C." Maxine was refilling a man's coffee cup at the counter.

"She could walk by a cemetery and raise a dead man right out of the ground," Merle said.

Maxine put the coffeepot on the burner and came around the counter to their table. "What for you boys?"

"I've got something for you, baby," L.C. said.

She put one hand on her hip. Puffing out her lower lip, she blew strands of hair out of her eyes. "What do you want, L.C.?"

"You know what I want."

"Ain't on the menu."

L.C. pulled his cap low over his eyes. "Well, it sure has been on the menu before."

Merle put his arm around Zeb. "Hey, Maxine, know who this is?"

"Billy the Kid?"

"This is our brother, Zeb," said L.C. "He's a musician."

"Merle got the looks, he got the talent—where does that leave you, L.C.?"

Smiling and winking at her, L.C. put his hand between his legs.

"I wouldn't give you a nickel for what you're holding."

"You sure are sassy tonight."

"I'm tired, my feet hurt, and I've got a low threshold for bull-shit. Now what do you all want besides trouble?"

Zeb and Merle asked for draft beers.

"L.C.?"

L.C. motioned for Maxine to come closer. She leaned over him, and he whispered something in her ear. She snatched off his cap, slapped him with it, threw it on the floor, and walked off.

"She's wild about me," L.C. said, picking up his cap.

"Sure she is," said Merle.

"She loves me, she just don't know it yet." L.C. put his cap back on his head and grinned at Zeb. "Welcome home, brother."

Later that night as he lay in bed, Zeb pictured L.C. in his Army uniform, looking like a zombie as the automatic rifle jerked in his hands, the spent shells spinning away like brass teardrops. He remembered reading about a massacre of Vietnamese people and thinking the soldiers had gone crazy. He'd had no idea L.C. had been involved in such a thing. L.C. has been back from the war for five years, and all that time he has been living with the guilt for what happened. His first year back from 'Nam, L.C. hadn't done much. He had spent a lot of time hanging around Yancy's Bar and Pool Hall or driving the back country roads in his truck. Jadine said he walked in his sleep. She found a bag of pot in his room and gave him hell, crying and praying over him. It had taken him weeks to convince her he wasn't a drug addict just because he smoked a little weed now and then.

L.C. had eventually gotten his life together. He got a job as a mechanic at Gil's Gulf down on Main Street, and Gil later promoted him to assistant manager. Then L.C. bought a half interest in Gil's Wrecker Service and started making money out the wazoo. He even bought himself a house, on Chinaberry Street behind the Seaton Tobacco Market. He sure seemed to be doing all right for himself.

But he's still carrying around all that guilt, Zeb thought. He wondered if L.C. still walked in his sleep.

The next morning Zeb sat between Merle and Jadine in Gibbons Baptist Church, trying to concentrate on the preacher's sermon, but he was soon distracted by a young woman sitting in front of him. Her nape, hair, and ear bore a striking resemblance to the same section of his wife's anatomy. He wondered if the stranger's ears turned red when she became sexually aroused. He was pondering this question when the congregation stood up to sing a hymn, "Can the Lord Depend on You?" Zeb didn't stand up at first, not until after both Jadine and Merle had nudged him with their elbows. He pressed against the back of the pew, trying to conceal his miserable, wicked tumescence.

Four

Lavis first saw Zeb's mother Jadine in a tent revival in a field out-side of Seaton. He was twenty-two, she was seventeen. He kept staring at her while the sweating preacher worked the crowd. She got away before he could find out who she was or where she had come from. He didn't see her again until the summer morning two years later when he passed her on the sidewalk in front of the Seaton Post Office. He followed her two blocks before he got up enough nerve to ask her name. As an opening ploy Lavis said she looked exactly like his cousin Sarah in Florida, and did she have any kin there? That's how he learned she was visiting her aunt in Seaton. When he asked if he could come see her, Jadine must have been taken aback, but she said yes. She told Zeb later how Lavis had appeared on her aunt's porch the next afternoon, holding a bunch of daisies, his hair slicked down, his shoes shined. He sat on the porch awhile with his legs crossed, not saying much except, "Would you like to see an alligator?" He returned the next day and drove her out to the Choctoosie in an old truck that smelled like fish.

Jadine told Zeb she never saw the alligator, she wasn't sure there was one. She liked Lavis, however, although she suspected he might be somewhat unmanageable.

That fall he began going down to see her at her family's home-place in Holden County, which bordered Sumner County to the south. He would ride down on his father's mule since Elkins needed the truck. Lavis would hang around her parents' farm, working for nothing, sometimes spending the night in their barn. Once when Lavis was drinking with Oscar Deloatch, Zeb over-heard him tell Oscar how he had lain in the straw thinking of

Jadine. "I looked up through the barn door, and there she'd be in the window, undressing for bed. She's stretch, take off some more of her clothes, and then maybe stop and brush her hair. I'd get so hot many a night I thought about fucking the mule."

Zeb wondered if Lavis had ever screwed the mule. He imagined a creature wandering in Wildcat Swamp, half Dupree, half mule, with a head resembling the old man, only misshapen and ugly with a furry body. He dreamed he stumbled onto this creature while hunting and shot it between its crossed eyes, putting it out of its lonesome misery.

Lavis and Jadine were married a year after his first visit to her parents' farm, and they lived for a summer and fall with Jadine's parents. Lavis worked for her father, Joel Price, who farmed and owned a feed-grinding mill. Lavis soon grew tired of working for his father-in-law, however, and he and Jadine packed up and moved to Seaton where Lavis got a job repairing farm equipment. He had a knack for fixing engines. Farmers brought him their trucks, tractors, and cars for repairs. They would give him a few drinks of whiskey, flatter him while he worked, and he would often forget to charge them, no matter how strapped he was for money. Lavis didn't stay at the tractor company long before he started sharecropping on the Grant Clayton farm on the Alsace Highway. Zeb was the first-born, and then eighteen months later, L.C. Merle was born two years after L.C.

When Zeb was four they moved onto Rainy Bowden's farm on Highway 11, four miles south of Seaton. The ninety-acre farm had a two-story frame house with a tin roof, a barn, an outdoor toilet, and a curing barn for the tobacco. A dirt road ran past the barn and around through the field to the log tobacco barn.

The front door of the house opened onto a hallway which ran back to the living room. Soon after they moved into the house Lavis installed a sink at the back of the hallway, and he ran a hose from the sink to a large washtub where everyone bathed. A few years later he brought home a cast-iron tub, with lions' paws for feet, and set it up near the sink, cutting a hole into the floor for a drain. An Oriental screen provided privacy. The hall wasn't heated, and in the winter cold air blew in from around the door.

The farm owner and Lavis were closely linked in Zeb's memory, although they were quite different. Rainy Bowden was fat and loud, whereas Lavis was lean and soft-spoken. Rainy, who owned more than a thousand acres in Sumner County, spent his days riding around in his truck, overseeing his farms, drinking whiskey, and bullshitting. Zeb considered Rainy to be a champion bullshit artist. For example, he was forever promising Lavis he would have a bathroom installed in the house after the fall harvest, but he never did. The old man never had the guts to complain.

Rainy was always dreaming up new schemes to make money, like raising rabbits or blueberries or digging out a pond in the hollow behind the hog lot and raising catfish. Whenever he visited the farm, he would drive up in the yard, honk his horn, and wait for Lavis to come out. Lavis would sit in Rainy's truck, drink his whiskey, and listen to him run his mouth. When he came back in he would say something like, "Rainy Bowden is crazy if he thinks he can make money off catfish. There's a river full of catfish not twelve miles from here where a man can catch all he wants."

Rainy provided the house, land, and capital for fertilizer, crop chemicals, and seeds. Lavis supplied the labor and tractor. In the fall, after the crops were sold, Rainy subtracted Lavis' half of the expenses for fertilizer and seed from the total revenue. Lavis and Rainy divided the profit fifty-fifty. Before Lavis received any money, however, Rainy subtracted whatever amount he had advanced them to live on during the year. Lavis' final share of the profit was never more than ten thousand dollars, and it was usually less.

Tobacco brought in more money than the other crops combined. In late winter they would plant the tobacco seeds in beds behind the barn, pegging sheets of cheesecloth over the beds to protect the seedlings. When the plants were six inches or so high, they would transplant them to the field. Later that summer they would go through the tobacco and pull off the tendrils, or "suckers," that grew between the leaves. And when the white blossoms appeared they would pinch them off, too, since they drew nourishment away from the leaves. They hunted the horned tobacco worms, tearing off their heads or stomping on them. If there was a dry spell Lavis would roll the wooden barrels out of the barn, fill them with water, put them on the wagon, and haul them out to the tobacco plants behind his tractor. Zeb, Merle, and L.C. watered the tobacco with buckets dipped into the barrels.

If black shank or blue mold attacked the tobacco leaves, or if they were damaged by hail, Lavis would usually go on a drunk.

The Hogans, a black family who lived on one of Rainy's other farms, helped harvest the tobacco. They were Josh and Myra and their children, Plato, Ragus, and Eula. Plato and Ragus were older than Zeb, Eula a year younger. Lavis would haul the wagon between the rows of tobacco while they pulled off the sturdiest leaves from the bottom of the plants and put them on the wagon. Then they would take the tobacco to the curing barn where they would tie the leaves to tobacco sticks, twenty-five to thirty clumps per stick. They hung the sticks across the tiers in the curing barn. Merle and Eula, being the lightest, worked up on the tiers. The rest of them formed a line and handed the sticks of tobacco up to them, the dew-wet leaves rustling like satin.

They cured the tobacco seven days over the flue, until the leaves turned gold, and then Lavis would take them to the Seaton Tobacco Market. There the farmers stacked their tobacco in bundles on the concrete floor. While the auctioneer, warehousemen, farmers, and buyers moved between the rows, the auctioneer chanting prices, Zeb, L.C., and Merle crouched behind the bundles, listening to the rhythmic flow of words. The auctioneer's voice echoed and rang as if in a cave.

About every two or three months Jadine's parents would visit. Whenever Grandpa Joel came to visit, a magpie would roost in the peach tree beside the garden. Grandpa Joel was tall and thin like a stove pipe, with a long, gray-black beard, deep-set melancholy eyes, and a voice that sounded like someone talking from down in a well. Grandma Beulah was short and ruddy, with a square jaw and a shrill, jolly laugh. Once Zeb asked his grandpa about the magpie. He said it was the spirit of his first wife, which had taken the form of a magpie. He took off his felt hat and thumped it with his palm, sending up a cloud of dust. "Ain't no use to drive her away," he said, "she'll only be back."

Jadine told Zeb that as a young man her father had been "a wild, hell-raising sinner." Then one night while he was asleep a tornado had ripped off the roof of his house, snatched him into the air, and dropped him in the branches of a chinaberry tree a quarter of a mile away. When Zeb asked his grandfather about the tornado, he said, "I still have dreams about that devilish thing. Felt like I'd been snatched up by a big hand and flung into the sky. And the noise—it was like a million souls crying out from the fiery pit."

Jadine said Joel got saved after his experience with the tornado, married Beulah, and settled down to live "a good Christian life."

When Zeb was eight years old, Joel and Beulah died in a head-on collision on their way home from church. The other motorist, a minister fleeing to Florida with his church's treasury, suffered only a broken collarbone. It was later revealed that the minister was guilty of knocking up a fourteen-year-old member of his congregation. The girl's parents had sent her to the preacher for help, claiming she had been possessed by the Devil. The preacher put her into a trance, and then violated her. She remembered what the preacher had done to her after her belly began to swell.

Lavis often cited the circumstances of Joel and Beulah's deaths as incontrovertible proof there was no justice to be found anywhere on earth.

For a year after the loss of her parents, Jadine could frequently be seen standing by the kitchen window, looking outside as if she were waiting for them to drive up. Once Zeb heard his father tell Oscar Deloatch she was taking her grief too seriously. Being as Joel and Beulah were killed coming home from church, Lavis guessed they were most likely in heaven. He, on the other hand, figured he would go to hell after he died since he hadn't set foot in a church since 1949.

Lavis believed Jadine was going to inherit a large sum of money from her parents' estate. He bragged they were going to buy a farm and take a vacation in Florida. Although Jadine's parents did own a sizeable farm, it had been heavily mortgaged. Also, she had two brothers and a sister. When the estate was settled, her share amounted to six thousand dollars. Lavis bought a new truck and sent everyone to the dentist. Jadine got a television, refrigerator, and stove, and new wallpaper for the kitchen. For a while they all felt rich.

But the money ran out without any of them ever getting to see Florida.

After her parents died Jadine began going to church more often and making sure her sons went to Sunday school. They were too young to offer much resistance. They attended Gibbons Baptist on the Alsace Highway. The folks at Gibbons Baptist took life seriously, frowning on dancing, card playing, and, especially, drinking alcohol. On all those Sunday mornings Zeb had to get up and attend church with Jadine, how he envied Lavis, who got to lie in bed, putter at his workbench, or, better yet, go fishing. The congregation at Jadine's church was mostly "a bunch of tight-assed old hypocrites," according to Lavis. "They're so busy studying how they can beat someone out of a dollar or else hurt somebody for no reason, that they're wasting their time praying. Good Lord ain't paying them any mind."

When Zeb was eleven he was baptized in the Choctoosie River. He remembered crouching down in the water, his feet sinking into the mud. Then hands seized him, lifted him up, and in a burst of light he saw the preacher, his face framed by sparkling drops of water, his mouth and eyes opened wide. In each blue iris there was a miniature cross around which was coiled a snake. "Baptized in the name of Jesus," the preacher cried that day, "washed in the precious blood of the lamb!" And then Zeb was struggling through mud and water toward the riverbank where people were singing and Jadine was reaching down to take his hand.

Five

Zeb was driving on a country road west of Cedar Springs, looking for a house to rent when he passed a flatbed truck pulled off onto the side of the road, legs sticking out from underneath. He pulled off the road and walked back to the truck. "Can I give you a hand?"

"Hand me that wrench, will you?" A woman's voice. A slim hand pointed to a wrench on the pavement, next to a pack of Camels.

He knelt beside her, handing her the wrench. "What's the trouble?"

"Gas line is clogged, rings are bad, got a burnt cylinder, a bad battery, and I think the generator is shot." She worked under the truck a minute with the wrench, then scooted out. She had a thin face, straight brown hair, high cheek bones, wide-set gray eyes. Grease on her nose and chin. She wore jeans, brogans, and a denim jacket over a flannel shirt.

"Think you can fix it all up with that wrench?"

She brushed a wisp of hair out of her eyes, leaving a smear of grease on her forehead. "I was just working on the fuel line. That's the one thing I can fix."

"Sounds like you need a mechanic."

"I need more than a mechanic." She stood up and kicked a tire. "Going north?"

"Yeah."

"Can I catch a ride?"

"Sure."

She rolled back under the truck and gathered up her wrenches, then they walked to his truck.

"I haven't had anything but trouble with that damn truck since I got it," she said, when she got into his truck. She smelled of wood smoke and gasoline. "Oh, look at the puppy. What's his name?"

"Henry." Zeb pulled onto the road.

She took the pup out of the cardboard box on the seat and held him in her lap. "Hello there, Henry. What a cute puppy you are. And only one eye. But it's a pretty eye. All big and brown."

"Do you know of any houses around here for rent?" he asked.

"No, I had to look for months before I found mine. Been looking long?"

"Just since yesterday. I'd been renting a room in town, but the manager found out I had a puppy, and he kicked me out."

"Oh, he's licking my fingers. Henry, you're just a little ball of love, aren't you?" She put the puppy back in the box, and took out a pack of Camels. "Cigarette?"

"No, thanks."

"Mind if I smoke?"

"No."

After a few miles she asked him to pull off the road in front of a small frame house with a tin roof, and an outhouse and shed out back. She jumped out as soon as the truck stopped, then bent down to look in the window. "Thanks for the ride."

She ran up to the house before he could ask her name.

Three nights later he was standing on a crowded dance floor in the Electric Cat, and he saw her among the dancers. The lights were flashing—red, green, yellow, blue—and the musicians were writhing up on stage, their electronic rhythms driving the dancers into a frenzy. She appeared in this phantasmagoria, armed raised, hips gyrating, then vanished into the swirling crowd.

He looked for her the rest of the night, but couldn't find her in the crowd.

"Any luck finding a fiddling job?" Sloe Gin asked.

"Not yet. Right now I'm trying to find a place to live. I got thrown out of my room because of my pup."

"Where you been sleeping?"

"Back of my truck."

"It's supposed to rain tonight. Come on into the Saloon around closing time, and you can sleep on one of the pool tables."

"Thanks."

He awoke suddenly and sat on the side of the pool table, trying to shake the dream from his mind. He had come home to his apartment in New Orleans and found Roseanne in bed with her lover.

The jukebox glowed in the corner. Sloe Gin had forgotten to unplug it. Zeb played an Otis Redding song, "I've Been Loving You Too Long." He sat on the side of the pool table, sipping whiskey from a pint he had in his suitcase and listening to Otis sing. He kept playing the song again and again. After he finished the pint, he got the idea of calling the reverend.

He called him from the pay phone in the breezeway.

"Mr. Lamar, I'm sorry to disturb you. I need to get in touch with Roseanne."

"Zebulon? Do you know what time it is?"

"No, sir, but I've got to talk to Roseanne. Could I have her number, please?"

"Leave her alone. She's trying to make a new life for herself."

Zeb pictured the reverend's florid face: a huge tropical flower. "I still love her, Mr. Lamar."

"You're not capable of love."

"Give her a message for me, please. Tell her I—"

"Zebulon, you're an irredeemable bum!"

The metal pay phone was cold against Zeb's face as he stood there listening to the dial tone. Roseanne's father had said he was a bum with such authority—a voice from a burning bush. He pictured the reverend sitting at the head of his table, devouring food. He was big as a blimp, this man of God. Back in the summer, when Zeb and Roseanne had last visited Seaton, the reverend had summoned him to his study for a talk.

"Zebulon," he had said, in a booming, ministerial voice, "we're worried about you."

"Why?"

"You're abusing your body with alcohol, you're withdrawn and depressed, and you're unemployed. Is that any way to treat our beloved Roseanne?"

"No, sir, it isn't."

The reverend shifted his huge body in the chair. The folds of his face moved in and out as he breathed, like an accordion.

"This is a dangerous time for you, son. You've recently experienced a profound tragedy, the untimely death of your father. Grief makes us weak, confused. Satan is cunning, he knows when we are most vulnerable, and he has an awesome power to beguile a confused mind. Do not forget that Lucifer was the most beautiful of the angels."

"I'll try to remember that, sir."

Mrs. Lamar had been even less charitable. When she spoke to Zeb at all, it was in a dreadful, croaking whisper, as if she were communicating with a voice from the dead.

Returning to the pool table, Zeb rummaged through his suitcase until he found a small box of snapshots. He sat on the side of the table and looked at photos of Roseanne on their wedding day, in Key West on their honeymoon, and in New Orleans. He lingered over one photo of Roseanne, linking arms with a toothless old man on the levee during Mardi Gras. She was smiling and her hair was in braids. She wore jeans and a tight T-shirt which showed off her lovely breasts.

Zeb remembered his dream, and he put his face in his hands.

"I'm going to kill him," he told Henry, who was staring at him from his cardboard box in the corner. "Does he know he's fucking with a man whose great-great uncle used to ride with Jesse James?"

During rush hours at Lorenzo's, on Friday and Saturday nights, Zeb, Uriah, and H. T. could never get the dishes washed quickly enough to satisfy Lorenzo. Often when they were working the hardest, he would shout at them to work faster and accuse them of wasting time. After one particularly hectic weekend, Uriah missed two days of work. When he returned, Lorenzo bawled him out in front of Zeb and H. T.

"I'm sick and tired of bums like you, Uriah. Running a business in America is hard enough without having to worry about slimeballs, ingrates, and people who don't take their work seriously. Turn in your apron. You're fired!"

Lorenzo glared at Uriah as the old man slowly took off his apron and hung it on a nail in the corner. Then Lorenzo stalked out of the kitchen.

"Don't pay him no mind, Uriah," H. T. said. "He nothing but a big, empty-headed fool."

Zeb and H. T. shook Uriah's hand and wished him luck.

"Where are you going now, Uriah?" Zeb asked.

The old man shrugged, smiled. "Whichever way the wind blows."

"I was hoping you'd stick around long enough to teach me the names of all the dishes."

"You look at them as long as I have, you'll recognize them," Uriah said.

Zeb had the next day off. In the afternoon, he took a bottle of wine down to Uriah's room and knocked on the door. A stranger answered. "I just rented this room," he said. "I don't know nobody named Uriah."

Zeb went down to the Saloon and ordered a beer at the bar. It was just after five PM, and the carpenters, painters, and electricians were coming in. Soon Duane sat down on the next stool.

He nodded at Zeb, and Zeb asked him if he knew of anything to rent in the country.

"Only thing I know about is a bus."

"Where is it?"

"Out on Turtle Creek Road, not far from where I live. Follow Jefferson Street on out of town, heading west. After you cross the lake, you'll be on Pine Top Road. Go about five miles then turn right at the Texaco Station, that's Turtle Creek Road. After a couple of miles you'll see a junkyard on the left. The bus is behind the junkyard. Ask in the office for Tick Cogswell."

"He own the bus?"

"He owns the whole plantation," Duane said.

Zeb turned into the gravel road leading into the junkyard. To the left was a concrete block building with a faded sign over the door: *Cogswell Salvage Company*. Two black boys were sitting on an engine block by the door. Zeb rolled down the window and asked them where he could find Tick Cogswell.

"Drive on into the junkyard," one boy said. "You'll see his place on the right."

The road into the junkyard curved around through the smashed, twisted cars. Rusted car parts were strewn about like bones. Off to his right, at the end of a driveway, was a double-wide trailer surrounded by a white picket fence. A pickup truck and a Pontiac sedan were parked in the driveway.

A short, stocky man with gray hair answered the door.

"Mr. Cogswell?"

"That's right."

"Name's Zeb Dupree. Heard you have a bus for rent."

The man stepped out onto the porch. He wore a flannel shirt, jeans, cowboy boots, and a belt buckle bearing the inscription *The West wasn't won with a registered gun.* "You a student?"

"No, sir. I work in Cedar Springs."

"You any kin to Snake Dupree?"

"Not that I know of."

"Where you from?"

"Seaton. Down east."

"This Dupree was from around here. He's in the state pen now. They got him for cattle rustling."

"I don't believe we're any kin," Zeb said.

"What kind of work you do?"

"Restaurant work." Through the door Zeb could see a green parrot in a cage.

"Well, come on, and I'll show you the bus."

They walked out through the driveway, following the road down through the junkyard.

"I bought the bus from a musician, after his band broke up," Tick said. "Had a wench living with me at the time, and I needed a little place where I could get off by myself, maybe play a little poker, or just turn up the radio real loud. I fixed it up for that purpose, but me and her parted before I had a chance to use it much."

The silver bus rested on concrete blocks in a stand of pines behind the junkyard. Painted on the side was *The Spaghetti Brothers Blues Band.* Tick had divided the bus into two rooms. The front section contained a range, sink, and refrigerator; the rear section had a cot in it and a tiny bathroom with a shower. The bus was full of windows, every one with a blue curtain.

47

"I put an oil furnace in to keep her warm in the winter," Tick said.

"I like it," Zeb said. "How much is the rent?"

"Seventy-five a month."

"I've got a dog."

"Junkyard ought to have a dog. Been meaning to get one myself."

"I'd like to rent it. You need any references?"

"That won't be necessary. You seem like a decent fellow."

"If you have a pen, I can write you a check now."

"Come on up to the house."

They left the bus and walked back through the junkyard.

"That wench I had living with me was a curiosity," Tick said. "I picked her up hitchhiking one day, and she told me the saddest story, all about how her mom had died when she was born, and how her daddy had recently been killed in a car accident. She was just traveling around the country, sleeping wherever she could find a place. She asked me if I had a barn or a shed she could stay in a couple of days. I told her she could stay in my house. She was pretty as a june bug in a tin tipper, only about eighteen years old. I was just getting used to having her around when the Sheriff took her away in handcuffs. She was wanted for murder up in Ohio. She signed a confession the next day. Guess who she'd killed?"

"Who?"

"Her dear old daddy she'd told me so much about."

"Why'd she do that?"

"Well, she said they'd had trouble ever since she was little, but evidently the thing that set it off was a fight over the television. He took her TV privileges away from her, and she got his gun out of the bedroom and shot him right through the heart while he was watching *The Six Million Dollar Man.*" Tick shook his head. "I'm glad I let her watch all the TV she wanted."

"Lucky for you." Zeb noticed a nude doll leaning against the front bumper of a Dodge Desoto, one eye closed, its hand raised as if giving a benediction. He wondered if someone had put it there as a joke.

He followed Tick up the steps and into the double-wide.

"Hello, fag face," the parrot said.

"This is Baby."

"Hello, asshole."

"I got her from a long distance trucker. She picked up most of that trashy language from him."

"Nice tits, nice tits."

"How'd your girlfriend and Baby get along?"

"Made each other jealous."

While Tick went to look for a pen, Zeb went up to the cage and looked at the parrot. "How you doing, Baby?"

"Let the good times roll," Baby said.

Cedar Springs had changed since he had been a student there, Zeb noticed, as he walked down Jefferson Street, looking at this year's students. They were clean-cut and wholesome-looking—future young Republicans. In front of the post office he saw a pledge for some fraternity: down on his knees, growling and barking. He wore paint-smeared rags, a mop wig, and a dog collar around his neck. A group of fraternity men stood nearby, smirking.

The pledge lunged at Zeb, growling.

"Stand up and be a man!" Zeb said.

"The cars," someone shouted, "go after the cars!"

The young man crawled into the street and began barking at the cars.

Jesus, Zeb thought, that's America's *future* out there.

Zeb and H. T. had their arms deep in dishwater when Lorenzo came into the kitchen to tell Zeb he was fired.

"You got a bad attitude, Dupree. I've had my eye on you. I came in here three times this week and caught you laughing on the job."

"You mean the man can't laugh if he feels like it?" H. T. asked.

"You stay out of this, H. T."

Zeb took off his apron and dropped it on the floor. "You're an asshole, Lorenzo. And you wouldn't be shit without your mama's money."

"Listen, Dupree, I'm an ex-Marine."

"So what? You're still an asshole."

Lorenzo's face was flushed. "If you're not out of here in thirty seconds I'm calling the cops."

He kicked the swinging doors open as he left the kitchen.

"Whooeeee!" H. T. said.

"Sorry to leave you with all these dirty dishes, H. T."

"It's worth it to hear you tell that fool off."

"I'd better be going."

"So long, Zeb. I'll get your check from Lorenzo and bring it by your bus."

"Thanks."

Zeb drove down to the Saloon where he ordered a tequila from Sloe Gin. He put it down fast and asked for another.

Sloe Gin was looking through the records by the bar's stereo. "Any requests, Zeb?"

"Got any old-time music?"

"Bill Monroe, the Stanley Brothers, the Blue Sky Boys."

"Put on the Blue Sky Boys."

Zeb sat there drinking tequila, listening to the old music he had heard when he was growing up, songs like "Don't This Road Look Rough and Rocky," "Tramp on the Street," and "Behind These Prison Walls of Love." He remembered playing these tunes at night on the front porch while the old man sat in the rocker. He could close his eyes and hear Lavis talking as he drove Zeb out to his old homeplace on the river.

"Rainy says I'm getting old, losing my strength, but I've got more strength now than I ever had. Feel the muscle in that arm, Zeb, ain't it just like a rock? Look at Rainy's arm sometime. Soft as a woman's. Man don't do nothing except ride around in his truck. But I've been working hard all my life, that's why I'm strong and he's weak. I was ploughing with a mule by the time I was eight years old, raising crops on our land by the river. That land was so rich you could throw a handful of watermelon seeds out the back door and before long you'd be ass-deep in watermelons. There was walnut trees and apple trees on our farm and every kind of animal you could name—bobcats, deer, coons, jack rabbits, and bears, too. This was back before the dragline and the bulldozer had started destroying the bears' kingdom. I remember one old bear we called "Sam Crockett." Sam had tore up every pack of dogs that had ever been sent into the swamp after him. He had been shot half a dozen times but he always survived. He was a pure legend. Stayed back in Wildcat Swamp mostly, in his kingdom. But

when he got ready to go somewhere he'd take to the road just like a man. And, Zeb, there was still some panthers back then, too. They'd scream at night and that sound would raise chill bumps all over my body. But they killed off all the panthers, and now they're killing off the bears. Before long there won't be nothing wild left. All the wild animals will be dead or in the zoo."

"How about another shot?" Sloe Gin asked.

"Sure."

As Sloe Gin poured him another shot of tequila, Zeb had a sudden recollection of the girl whose truck had broken down on the highway: there had been something unusual about her eyes.

They'd had specks of gold in them.

Someone woke him up next morning, pounding on the door of the bus.

It was Duane, his first visitor.

"I just stopped by to see if you got moved in O.K."

"Hey, Duane. Come on in."

Duane came into the bus and sat down on the couch. Besides the couch there was also a card table, two folding chairs, and a bookshelf. Zeb had decorated the walls with a 1956 calendar of pin-up beauties, a poster of Bill Monroe and the Bluegrass Boys, and an old photograph of Lavis and Jadine, taken soon after they were married.

"Cozy place," Duane said.

"How about some coffee?"

"Good idea."

Zeb filled up a kettle with water and put it on the stove, then sat on the couch.

"You look a little rough," Duane said.

"Got fired yesterday. Took the rest of the day off and got drunk."

"Why'd you get fired?"

"Laughing on the job. Boss said I had a bad attitude."

"What kind of reason is that to fire someone?"

"It was a shit job, anyway."

"Got anything else lined up?"

"No. I've got some money in the bank, though."

"I could use some help painting condos."

"I'm unskilled labor."

"It's not that hard to learn."

"I can't believe it, a job offer before coffee. Must be my lucky day."

"What made you decide to move here?"

"I went to school here, so I had some good memories about the town. After my marriage broke up in New Orleans, I decided to come back here and find a job playing in a string band. There were a lot of them around back when I was in college."

Duane said he had moved to Cedar Springs from Austin, Texas three years earlier with his girlfriend, Lisa.

"She came here to get her MBA. I put her through the program, painting houses. After she graduated she said her feelings for me had changed. She said, 'I love you Duane, but the painful truth of the matter is I just need a man with more ambition than you've got.' She's in D.C. now, an investments analyst, whatever the hell that is."

"You got your own business, Duane. You could end up making more than she does."

"I doubt it. I'm just trying to get by. Got a little house near the river, a garden out back, a couple of hogs and some chickens. I like the simple life. A cold beer, a plate of barbecue, a good tune."

"Bring your guitar over sometime. We'll play some tunes."

"I've got my old Gibson in the truck. Want to hit a lick or two?"

"Sure," Zeb said. The kettle was whistling. "Let me fix the coffee."

When Duane returned with his guitar, Zeb had two mugs of instant coffee ready on the table. He got his fiddle out, and they tuned up together, then launched into "Cotton-Eyed Joe." Next they played "Leather Britches," "Lazy Liza," and "Blackberry Blossom." They played a jazz number, then some hornpipes and reels. Duane kept a good steady rhythm, leaving Zeb to weave in and out of the beat.

"You should be playing in a band," Duane said.

"I could say the same about you."

"I wouldn't mind playing in a band again, as long as I didn't have to go on the road. I like to be home at night where I can hear the river."

"Where do you live?"

"Go down Turtle Creek Road a couple of miles, turn left at the big pine. Cross the river, it's the first house on the right."

"You own the place?'

"Me and the bank. House plus five acres."

"I met a girl who lives on down this road a few miles. Drives a flatbed truck. You know her?"

"I don't believe so. Why?"

"I just wondered," Zeb said.

That night he got a lantern, his fishing poles, a tackle box, and a can of chicken livers, and he drove down to the Pocahontas Bridge, which spanned the Little Fork River near where Duane lived. He pulled off the road just past the bridge and walked down a path to the water. He lit the lantern and rigged up stands for the fishing poles, using Y-shaped branches he cut from a sapling. He put weights on the lines, baited the hooks with chicken livers, and cast them into the river. He didn't put any floats on the lines, so the bait could go all the way to the bottom where catfish feed. Soon one of the poles bent down. He grabbed it and pulled up a small catfish. He hooked the stringer through its mouth, tied the stringer to a tree root, and dropped the catfish back into the water. He leaned back against a log, listening to the murmur of the river. He fell asleep on the bank and dreamed he was lost in Wildcat Swamp. The moon was full, the swamp drenched with fog. In a clearing he came upon a body hanging from a tree: it was Lavis. Zeb climbed the tree, cut down the body, and began carrying it on his back through the swamp. His bad leg was aching, and he was sinking down into the mud. He wondered how long he would be able to keep moving with the old man's weight on his back.

Six

His freshman year in high school, Zeb made the junior varsity football team. He had big plans. He dreamed of scoring the winning touchdown in the last game of the season between Seaton High's Wolverines and their ancient rivals, the Benton City Bears, in a battle for the Albemarle Sound championship. Although he worked as hard as the other honchos during practice, the coach only let him play twice that season. He still planned to get on the varsity team that fall.

But that summer he hurt his leg.

He and L.C. had bought a jar of moonshine from Weasel Yow, whose uncle had a still back in Wildcat Swamp. One afternoon while Jadine, Lavis, and Merle were in town shopping, Zeb and L.C. drank the moonshine behind the tobacco barn, chasing it with three bottles of R.C. Cola. After L.C. passed out, Zeb walked down the road to the house. The cock-eyed sun was sinking fast, the road swam before his eyes like a fish. He began singing.

> *What a friend we have in whiskey,*
> *all our sins and grief to bear.*
> *In the sweet embrace of moonshine*
> *we sail through life without a care.*

When he got to the barn there was the old man's John Deere, surrounded by a red haze. He climbed on, started up the engine, and drove the tractor down the road toward the tobacco barn. Veering to the left he gunned it along the edge of the field, then turned onto the roadbed that ran through the pines to the next field, the tractor lurching, careening. He zipped along the edge of the tobacco field, inhaling dust and tractor exhaust. He was the prince of speed, lord of the ground, the trees, the sky—suddenly the tractor rose up on its back wheels, and with a treacherous heave flipped over on its side, pinning him to the ground. He had tried to turn too fast on an incline. The metal bit deeply into his leg. He couldn't get his breath. As he lay there pissing and bleeding on himself he remembered Fergus Flynn, the preacher at Gibbons Baptist, saying you know neither the hour nor the minute the Angel of Death will come calling, so you had best be right with Jesus every minute of every day.

By the time Lavis found him he was out of his head, raving about the Devil.

That fall, when he wasn't in the hospital, he hobbled around Seaton High on crutches, his dreams of football glory ended. His buddies were a million laughs. He was now known as "Long John Silver" and "C. V." for Confederate Veteran. He knocked everyone out the morning he came to school wearing a black eye patch, a toy cutlass stuck in his belt. Despite his clowning around he was in a black gloom. He knew he would never get laid now that he was crippled and couldn't play football, couldn't even throw the shot put. The tractor had broken two ribs and crushed his left leg so badly he nearly lost it. His kneecap was demolished, his bones splintered and crushed. In a series of operations doctors rebuilt the kneecap and installed a metal pin in his lower leg. His leg often felt like a shark was chewing on it. Worse than the physical pain, however, was the knowledge that he would always walk with a limp.

At home Jadine nearly drove him crazy with her attention. One night, fed up with her pity, he threw a cup of hot chocolate at the television, all over Matt Dillon and Miss Kitty. Lavis, who had been watching the show, jumped up and punched him in the mouth, knocking him to the floor. Zeb pulled himself up and began cussing Lavis, daring him to hit him again. Lavis obliged him, this time knocking him over the couch. Then Jadine rushed in from the kitchen and began giving Lavis hell for hitting "a cripple."

Zeb struggled upstairs on his crutches, and lay on his bed listening to them going at it downstairs.

He wondered why he was living.

Roseanne Lamar first appeared in his life one sunny morning in September, a transfer student from Elizabeth City. She was the daughter of the Reverend Francis Lamar, the new pastor of Seaton's prestigious First Baptist Church. The morning she appeared in Miss Dovey Mathers' ninth grade homeroom, he tried to win her attentions with wild man antics, like his dramatic demonstration of a gorilla fighting two four-hundred-pound buzzards. His performances were in vain, however, for Roseanne only associated with rich kids, scions of old Sumner County families like the McCullochs, Wades, and Yardleys. Zeb hung around with L.C., Merle, and the Yow brothers, Andy and Weasel. The Yows were sharecroppers, too. Although he and Roseanne had some classes together, they rarely spoke. He often gazed at her in hallways, lunch lines, and classrooms. She was a triumph of Aryan evolution with her honey-colored hair, her lavender eyes, her perfect bubble ass. Her spread-eagled body glowed like a luminescent Christ in his mind while he lay drenched in the sweat of his sinning flesh. Being a redneck, and ugly and crippled to boot, he had about as much chance with her as a water moccasin had to stand up and sing "The Tennessee Waltz."

But you couldn't stop a man from dreaming.

Once, during their junior year, he earned the highest score on a difficult chemistry exam which most of the class had flunked. Afterwards, Roseanne turned around in the lunch line to smile and say, "There's Zeb, the wizard."

She was going out that year with David Grady, the surgeon's son. He would see them in the breezeway, David drooling, mooning, ass-over-heels in love.

In the fall of his junior year his English teacher, Mrs. Inez Macon, assigned the class a writing project—a theme on what they had done that summer. Zen thought the idea so stupid he considered turning in a blank paper. Instead, he wrote about how he had crippled his left leg. He described how he had gotten drunk and taken off on the old man's John Deere, and how, after the tractor had turned over on him, he had lain in the field thinking the Angel of Death had come calling for his spirit, but that his soul had already been stamped *Property of Satan*. He wrote about being so scared he pissed on himself, and he described the operations, the physical therapy, the pain. The summer had taught him, he wrote, the truth of what his father had been saying for as long as he could remember: "A man ain't got the chance of a pissant in hell to find any happiness, not in this life."

He figured he would get an "F" on the theme; he was surprised to get it back with a "B." Beneath the grade Mrs. Macon had written, "Well-written, honest, and moving. If not for the profanity, this theme would be worthy of an A."

That fall and winter Mrs. Macon assigned more themes, this time on books like *The Great Gatsby* and *Heart of Darkness*. Although he considered his themes to be mostly bullshit—about the eternal quest for beauty or the conflict between good and evil—Mrs. Macon generally gave them A's. The following year Mrs. Macon, who also taught senior English, encouraged him to send applications off to three universities.

"You need to learn a trade, boy," Lavis told him, "instead of dreaming about college. That's for rich kids."

But Jadine put a jar labeled *Zeb's college fund* in the kitchen cabinet and began filling it up with coins. Every time he looked at that jar of coins, he would marvel at his mama's faith. He believed he could do the work; the problem was, he couldn't visualize himself as a college student. As far as he knew no one in either Jadine's or Lavis's family had ever gone to college. Jadine's relatives were mostly farmers or merchants. According to Lavis the Dupree clan in Virginia had produced a number of outlaws. Lavis claimed his great Uncle Hyatt Dupree had once ridden with Jesse James. Hyatt died of a shoot-out with the police in St. Louis, Missouri in 1886.

In the fall of Zeb's senior year his teachers nominated him for a scholarship that had been set up in the 1940s by Elisha Beaumont, a textile magnate, to provide academically gifted students with an opportunity to attend his alma mater, Cedar Springs State University. The Beaumont Scholarship, one of the most coveted scholarships in the state, paid tuition, food, room expenses, and even provided some spending money. Only three winners were chosen from the nominees in each regional district, the determining factor being an interview by the scholarship committee.

Zeb wasn't feeling very hopeful that November morning when he took the bus to Cedar Springs for the interview. It took place in an ivy-draped building on campus. The scholarship committee asked him why he wanted to go to college. Zeb had prepared a speech, about how he wanted to make a lasting contribution to society, but when it came time to make his bogus presentation to the committee members, he couldn't do it. Instead, he started talking about Lavis. He told them his father had been a sharecropper for most of his adult life, and that he had always said unless you were born rich you didn't have any more chance than a pissant in hell to get anywhere in life. Zeb added that the old man's predictions had certainly come true for him, since all he had to show for his labor in the world was a drinking problem, a bad back, a mouthful of rotten teeth, and an old John Deere. "The main reason I want to attend college," he said, "is so I won't have to end up like him."

The committee members greeted this revelation with a long silence. Finally, one old gentleman asked if he had "a special area of interest."

Suddenly, Zeb was sweating under their gazes. He realized he had exposed his miserable, impoverished background to the distinguished committee members. They were probably wondering why Sumner County couldn't do any better than him.

"History," he said. "I have a special interest in history."

He took the bus home thinking he had blown his chance to be a Beaumont man.

Homecoming night he watched the principal, Jack Leland, crown Roseanne Homecoming Queen. Her breasts undulated beneath her white satin gown; her face was radiant in the lights of the football field. The band was booming, everyone was cheering. Her escort was Huis Yardley, scion of one of the county's richest families, grandson to Amos, who had ended up with Lavis's home place.

All that fall he fantasized about taking her to the senior prom.

In January, Mr. Leland stopped him in the hall, and asked him to report to his office immediately. Zeb followed him down the hall, wondering what he had done wrong. Did Leland know about the jar of whiskey he had brought to school in a lunch box and drunk in the restroom with Andy Yow? Afterwards he and Andy had gone into study hall, high as hawks. Sweat dripping from his armpits, Zeb sat in front of the principal's desk while Mr. Leland shuffled through some papers. Maybe his hair was too long. Or perhaps a teacher had reported him for cussing in the hall.

Mr. Leland handed him a letter.

"This is from the Beaumont Scholarship committee, Zeb. They've selected you as a winner from our district. We're very proud of you, son."

The principal had a long, complicated nose, broad at the base, fat in the middle, then tapering down at the end like a sweet potato. Unable to grasp the full significance of his words, Zeb found himself concentrating on the man's nose as the principal told him what a fine school Cedar Springs State University was and how he hoped he would live up to the honorable traditions established by past recipients. Zeb was thinking first of Roseanne, because he had heard she was going to Cedar Springs, and then of Huis Yardley, her current flame, who was also going there. He could see the three of them walking around the campus.

That night he lay in bed thinking about how he would be floating through four years at the university on a gold cloud of money, courtesy of Elisha Beaumont, who had once walked the earth rich as a Saudi prince but who was now moldering in a vault somewhere with worms crawling through his eye sockets. Winning the scholarship set him to thinking deeply about the nature of things. Up until then he had always accepted his father's negative view of life, but now he had clear evidence the old man was wrong. After all, wasn't this America, land of infinite possibilities?

Jadine was so happy about his good fortune, she cried, but Lavis complained that winning the Beaumont scholarship would give Zeb "the big head," making him think he was better than anyone else. Their relationship began deteriorating, and by summer they had become so estranged that they were using Jadine, L.C., and Merle as intermediaries. Merle would come into the house and say, "Zeb, Daddy wants you to help pull 'bacca tomorrow." And Zeb would say, "O.K. Find out when he wants me to start."

He gained enough confidence from winning the scholarship to revive his fantasy of taking Roseanne to the prom. One night he drank down six beers and got up enough nerve to dial her number. But when he heard her voice his guts turned to Jello, and he hung up.

He ended up taking Florine Swicket, whose main claim to attention among the Seaton High Romeos was her watermelon-sized breasts. Zeb liked her breasts. The problem with Florine was, her face disappeared into a pasty blob if he looked at it very long. She was an intense girl. The first semester of their senior year she filled up five notebooks with nothing but his name.

The senior design committee set the theme of the prom, "Hawaiian Night," decorating the auditorium with paper-mâché palm trees and a mural of the sun setting over the sea. The night of the prom he danced with Florine in the gym. The band played "When a Man Loves a Woman," and Florine's tears dripped down his neck.

He kept straining for glimpses of Roseanne.

Graduation night Zeb and Florine drove around the back roads guzzling beer and throwing the cans out the window at highway signs. Most of the graduating seniors had left for Nags Head for the weekend. He stayed behind so he could spend the night with Florine in the Andrew Jackson Hotel in Riverville, the county seat. She was leaving early the next morning for the mountains, where she had gotten a summer job as a camp counselor. As usual, she wouldn't let him enter her ("Not until we're engaged, Zeb!"), but instead of the customary hand job she gave him a spectacular consolation prize. Drunk on beer and this new sweet pleasure he lay there with the bed's "magic fingers" massage apparatus purring beneath him, watching her head bob up and down. Even as he moaned his gratitude he was thinking of Roseanne.

The year after Zeb graduated from Seaton High, Sumner County made a token attempt at integration under the "freedom of choice" plan. Although no white students chose to attend Seaton's black high school, George Washington Carver, about fifty Carver students transferred to Seaton High. The principal, Jack Leland, announced this transfer at a special assembly in the spring of Zeb's senior year. Leland talked first about Seaton High School's traditions of "dignity and honor," and then he talked about his great-grandmother. He remembered her telling him about how General Sherman's men had stormed through Georgia and the Carolinas during the Civil War, burning, plundering, and committing crimes too heinous to even mention. They burned her homeplace to the ground, forcing her to flee into the woods. She later found refuge in a barn, living with "snakes and mice and spiders." Leland said he hoped his great-grandmother's ordeal would serve as an inspiration for Seaton High in the fall: a fine Southern lady forced by fate to live under compromising circumstances but with her dignity and honor intact. At that point Arnie McCombs, a wise-ass who had been dozing through most of Leland's speech, woke up and asked, "Are we going to go to school with niggers?"

That summer, the Ku Klux Klan organized a rally in a field outside of Seaton. The Klansmen were either too weak or too lazy to raise their heavy wooden cross, which they had hauled in on a flatbed truck, so they hired two black men off the streets of Seaton to raise it, an event duly recorded by a photographer from *The Seaton Gazette*. The photo was later picked up by the wire services and printed in newspapers coast to coast. Zeb ran across the photo again his junior year in college, in a text for a history course called The Contemporary South. The photo showed only one of the men's faces. He looked like a black Christ, struggling up the hill at Calvary.

Seven

An icy rain began falling in December. It rained for three days, turning the junkyard into a sea of mud. Even after the rain stopped, the sky was Confederate gray, and the wind whistled and moaned through the junkyard like a mad witch.

"This is a scene out of hell," Duane said one afternoon, as he dropped Zeb off from work. "I don't see how you stand it."

"Guess I've gotten used to it. Want to come in for a beer?"

"I'd better ease on out of here. I don't want to fight that mud in the dark."

Zeb had been working for Duane for two weeks, painting the interiors of some condos that were going up outside of town. It was a monotonous job that required him to stand for hours in a small space, rolling paint onto a wall. While he painted, he would reminisce about the past. He recalled the long, lazy afternoons he used to spend on the levee, after he and Roseanne had sold their home in the suburbs and moved to the apartment off St. Charles. He remembered walking the streets of the Quarter, mingling with the musicians, artists, hookers, drag queens, beggars, runaways, and tourists. Although he was unemployed, he felt at peace in that tawdry environment. For the first time in his life, he felt he had nothing to prove. When he played his fiddle in Jackson Square the coins tossed into his case made a light, airy sound, like fairies pissing into a thimble.

But Roseanne was upset with him.

"Is playing fiddle on the streets what you really want to do with your life?" she demanded one afternoon. "And what about me? Last month I had a home and security. What do I have now except a cheap little apartment and a husband who hangs out on the streets all day like a common gypsy?"

"Roseanne, I'll find another job. I just need some time to relax, get my priorities straight again. We've got enough money in the bank to live a year or more."

"I'm not waiting that long."

Zeb had spent the next week wooing her. He took her out to eat; he bathed her by candlelight; he took her to the Cabildo to see Napoleon's death mask, to Antoine's to eat lobster, to Preservation Hall to listen to Kid Thomas' jazz band; he took her on a steamboat trip up the Mississippi; and he hired an artist to paint her portrait. She didn't like the portrait, nor did she seem particularly receptive to his efforts to rekindle the flame of romance. The only thing that seemed to interest her was a course she had enrolled in at the Lafayette School of Business, something to do with investments. Now what in the world was she interested in that for? Zeb had wondered.

"Look alive, Zeb," Duane said, "you been painting the same spot for five minutes."

"Sorry." Zeb put more paint on his roller and moved over to begin painting a new section of wall. He remembered the final scene at lunch, after he had confronted Roseanne with her mysterious absences during the afternoon and evening.

"You don't have to wonder where I've been going anymore, Zeb," she said. "I'm moving out."

The television set was blaring in the living room—two sets of competing couples trying to guess the names of a famous couple from the Bible. The winner was to receive a new color TV. Every time the couples guessed an incorrect answer, a buzzer gave them the raspberry.

"Roseanne," he said. "I want you to think about this some more."

Bleeeep, went the buzzer. It was followed by laughter.

"I have thought about it."

"Naomi and Ruth," said a voice. *Bleeeeep*. More laughter.

He turned off the television. Taking his wife's hand he led her into the den, where he sat her down on the couch. He knelt before her, told her he loved her, and asked her to reconsider her decision.

"Forget it, Zeb."

A darkness began to take shape.

"Baby, is there—someone else?"

She wouldn't look at him: a bad sign.

"Come on, tell me. Where have you been going after class?"

She raised her face. Her lovely, violet eyes were cold and hard.

"You can't blame him. It was over between us before I met him."

Sometime later, Zeb found himself wandering around Audubon Park, thinking he was holding a hand dealt from a deck he had somehow stacked against himself. But why? He put this question to a live oak, and when the tree failed to answer, he began beating it with his head and face.

The beating was interrupted by a hand on his shoulder.

"Excuse me." The hand belonged to a New Orleans policeman.

"What do you want?" Zeb's head ached. Blood trickled from a cut on his forehead, into his left eye.

"I'd like to ask you to stop beating your head against that tree."

"Why? There a law against it?"

"No." The policeman pointed to his left where a small crowd of wide-eyed children had gathered: blacks, whites, Hispanics, an Asian—a scene from a soft drink commercial. "But you're upsetting the children."

"Sorry."

Zeb fled the park like a thief.

Her lover's name was Brad Markham. He'd had the desk next to hers in her class, Investment Strategies. Their "friendship" had begun casually, Roseanne confessed later: coffee now and then, a movie. "I didn't want the affair to start, Zeb, but I was driven to it by desperation. Ever since your father died you've been on the skids. It's terrible to watch someone you love falling to pieces before your eyes. I felt like I had no one to turn to but Brad."

In his vulnerable, cuckolded condition, Zeb was easily duped by her sophistry: he could see how everything had been his fault.

He wept, begged her forgiveness.

Markham, who was divorced, worked in the mortgage department of a bank. Zeb met him when he came over to help her move some of her things into his place. Humiliated by the tears he had shed, Zeb was determined to endure this new torture with stoic grace. He greeted his wife's lover with a smile and a handshake.

Markham was tall and handsome, with wavy blond hair, a cleft in his chin, a set of perfect teeth. He had the smooth, confident manner of a mortician.

"Good to meet you, Mr. Dupree," he said. "I've heard a lot about you." Roseanne's lover wanted Zeb to know that, having experienced a marriage breakup, he understood how difficult things could be. "If you ever feel the need to talk," he said, flashing his beautiful teeth, "please call me at the office." And he gave Zeb his business card.

"Got a light?" the woman asked.

"No," Zeb said, "but I can buy you a drink."

"That's even better."

"What are you drinking?"

"Banana daiquiri."

He ordered her a banana daiquiri from the bartender.

"I feel like I know you." Slender and striking, she had heavily made up eyes and shiny black hair.

"You've waited on me before, at Eddie's Diner."

"I knew I'd seen you around." She was still holding the cigarette. "Looks like I could get a fucking light."

He got a pack of matches from the bartender and lit her cigarette.

"Thanks an awful lot. You look like, let's see, an Aquarius."

He shook his head.

"Aries?"

"Wrong again."

"What are you?"

"Pisces."

"A dreamer. What the hell, world is full of dreamers. Me, I'm an Aries. We make things happen."

"Like what?"

"I'm a dancer, and I'm moving to New York City next month where I plan to get a part in a Broadway musical."

"Congratulations in advance."

"What's your name?"

"Zeb."

"Listen, Zeb, I want you to come home with me tonight."

She lived in a basement apartment off Whitmore Street, near Eddie's Diner. Zeb followed her there in his truck. When she got to her apartment, she was all over him. "I'm going to fuck your eyes out."

But she stopped him after they were undressed.

"I can't go through with this."

"Why not?"

"It's your leg. I'm sorry, but I got this thing about cripples. I probably wouldn't feel this way if I wasn't a dancer. My family has always placed a high value on physical beauty." She sat up and reached for a cigarette. "Don't take it personal, O.K?"

Zeb got up and began putting on his clothes.

"You don't have to leave, Jed. You can sleep here, as long as you understand the ground rules."

"My name is *Zeb*," he said. "And I understand the situation perfectly."

Driving home, he pulled off onto the side of the road and fell on his knees to vomit in the snow. When he raised his head he saw an emaciated dog staring at him; he could see it clearly in the moonlight. He took a candy bar out of his coat pocket, and, tearing off the wrapper, he offered the candy to the dog. "Here, boy."

The dog howled—an eerie, terrified cry—and ran into the woods.

Zeb bent over, holding his stomach, and puked again.

The dog was still howling back in the pines.

Carrying the shotgun in the crook of his arm, he walked through the rows of junked cars, the pup at his heels. Many of the cars were missing fenders, hoods, doors. Windshields had been shattered into spider web designs. At the edge of the junkyard he saw a large pile of tires, along with the pile of hubcaps Tick had told him about. He flipped the safety off of his L.C. Smith, and, picking up one of the hubcaps, he sailed it over the field. He quickly lined up the bead between the barrels with the flash of silver. *Ka-booooom!*

To his left he saw Henry flying down the muddy path between the rows of cars.

He picked up another hubcap and sailed it out over the field.

Ka-booooooom!

He broke open the gun and replaced the spent shells with two new ones.

"Mister, you might hit one of those hubcaps if you let me throw it for you."

He turned to see one of the black boys who worked for Tick, standing behind him.

"Help yourself."

The boy picked up a hubcap and sailed it over the field.

Ka-booooom!

"Bull's eye!" The boy picked up another hubcap and cocked his arm, ready to sail it over the field.

Zeb stared at the denim sky, waiting. The world was reduced to a few simple elements: the field of broom sage, the black boy, the pile of hubcaps, the sky. What did anything else matter? He raised the shotgun, lining up the sight with the flash of silver.

Ka-booooooom!

"Roseanne's home," Jadine said.

She and Zeb were in the den, decorating the Christmas tree. The gingerbread man he was tying to a limb nearly slipped from his fingers. "Is that right?"

"Paola Deloatch saw her downtown on Tuesday, shopping with Mrs. Lamar. Ruby said Roseanne had put on right much weight."

"Food's rich in New Orleans." He took a tinsel angel from the ornament box and tied it to a limb.

"You going to call her?"

"I don't know."

"I wonder if her parents know what she's done."

As Zeb tied a star to the tree he pictured Roseanne naked: her mounds and curves, her long legs, her honey-colored fleece.

"It wasn't really love, was it?" Jadine asked.

"It was for me, Mama."

After he finished decorating the tree, he drove down to Gil's Gulf Station on Main Street. Main Street curved on around past the Seaton Tobacco Market on the right and ended a mile farther at Robert E. Lee Boulevard.

He found L.C. in the bay, working on a car. "Merry Christmas."

"Hey, Zeb, when did you get in?"

"This morning. Can you get off for a beer?"

"Sure, let me tell Gil."

L.C. went into the station, then he came outside and got into Zeb's truck. "Let's go to Yancy's."

"You get Mama anything yet?" Zeb asked, as he drove up the street. It was a week until Christmas. Plastic Santas, elves, and reindeer jiggled on wires strung between the streetlights and telephone poles.

"Me and Merle bought her a TV. We can put your name on the box, too."

"I'll pay you for my share."

"You can pay us later if you want."

"I can pay you. How much is it?"

"One third of it would come to about a hundred bucks."

Zeb took two fifties out of his wallet and passed them to L.C.

"Sure you can afford it?"

"Hell, yes."

L.C. folded up the money and put it in his pocket. "Me and Merle are going out to the cemetery this afternoon and put a wreath on Daddy's grave. Want to come?"

"Sure," Zeb said. But he didn't want to go.

At Yancy's, an old Elvis tune, "Young Dreams," was playing on the jukebox. Yancy stood behind the counter, munching on a pickled pig's foot. He was a tall, slouching man with yellow teeth, a pug nose, close-set eyes. Slumped on a stool at the back was one of Lavis's old drinking buddies, Daryl Jenks.

"Well, I'll be damned," Yancy said, when he saw Zeb.

"Say, Yancy." Zeb and L.C. sat at the counter and asked for draft Buds.

"Still married to the reverend's daughter?" Yancy asked, as he set the mugs on the counter.

"Sure."

L.C. threw a five-dollar bill on the counter. "How about some quarters for the jukebox."

Yancy took the bill and shuffled back to the cash register. The noise of the register jarred Daryl out of his alcoholic stupor.

"Hey, Zeb, L.C., how you boys doing today?"

They nodded at Daryl, whose eyes were filling up with tears.

"Lavis Dupree was the best friend I ever had."

"Shut up, Daryl," L.C. said.

Yancy put L.C.'s change on the counter. He stood there smirking, scratching himself between the legs. He was as ugly as a dead hog.

L.C. got up and went to the jukebox. Daryl was still blubbering.

"I'll be back in a minute, L.C.," Zeb called. He had to get out of there.

He called the reverend's house from the phone booth in front of the post office, across the street from Yancy's. Mrs. Lamar answered. The temperature of her voice dropped to below freezing when she heard who it was. "I'll see if she's in."

"Hello."

"Hey, it's me."

"I thought you might call."

"I called here once before."

"Daddy said you were drunk."

"He was a million laughs. He called me a bum."

"You shouldn't have called him when you were drinking, Zeb."

He rested his head against the pay phone. "Can I see you?"

"How about after Christmas?"

"I'd like to see you before then."

Roseanne sighed. "All right. I'll meet you somewhere for lunch."

"Where, when?"

"How about tomorrow at the Pier House, in Riverville?"

"O.K. What time?"

"Around one. I have to go now, Zeb."

"I'll see you tomorrow."

"Good-bye."

Zeb hung up the phone and watched Daryl Jenks come out of the front door of Yancy's. Daryl walked slowly down the sidewalk, his hands outstretched like a zombie in a horror movie.

Hank Williams was singing on the tape player as L.C. turned into the driveway of Gibbons Baptist Church. A light snow was falling. L.C. parked the truck, leaving the tape player on, and he,

Zeb, and Merle walked back to the cemetery. Merle carried the wreath. They stood around Lavis's grave with their heads bowed while Hank's voice floated over the tombstones. Hank was singing "I Can't Help It If I'm Still In Love With You." Zeb tried to say a prayer, but instead he remembered the preacher delivering Lavis's eulogy above the closed casket. The preacher's voice had been loud and tinny, like an out-of-tune piano.

It's a short walk from heaven to hell, he thought that night, as he lay upstairs in his old bed, listening to the rain on the tin roof. He had certainly felt like he was in heaven many times during the early days of his marriage. Although he had worked like a mule, knowing Roseanne was at home waiting for him had made all of his effort worthwhile. They had spent the first year of their marriage in Pine Grove, a town north of Raleigh, where Zeb had been a general assignment reporter for the county newspaper. Roseanne, who had majored in education, did substitute teaching in a private school. Every Friday afternoon they would celebrate pay day on pillows on the dining room floor beneath a chandelier Roseanne had ordered from an ad in *Southern Living*. After a year in Pine Grove, Zeb had gotten a job as an assistant editor of *The Bayou Journal* in suburban New Orleans. Eighteen months later, when the editor resigned to take another job, Zeb was promoted to editor, with a twenty-five percent raise. He and Roseanne bought a split-level home and a station wagon to haul around the children they planned to have. Roseanne went off the pill, and at night she sat around knitting baby clothes, reading books about pregnancy and caring for infants.

But her period kept coming. Regular as a factory whistle.

Zeb went to the doctor for a sperm count. He had millions of the little devils, with high motility. The doctor checked Roseanne and declared her to be fine. So what the hell was the matter? "Keep trying," the doctor advised. "Sometimes these things take time."

Roseanne began offering to babysit for the neighbors' children. She would meet Zeb in the door when he came home from work, holding a sullen child by the hand. "This is Jennifer," she'd coo, eyes full of mother love.

As the months passed, Roseanne began to grow listless and put on weight. She and Zeb began arguing over insignificant things. He started hanging around bars after work.

And then came the long distance call from the preacher at Gibbons Baptist:

"Zeb, you need to come home, son. There's been a terrible tragedy."

He heard footsteps on the stairs. It was Jadine, coming up to cover him with a quilt.

"Thanks, Mama."

"I didn't know you were awake."

"We went out to the cemetery today and put a wreath on Daddy's grave."

"I know."

"What happened that day, Mama?"

"I don't even know where to begin."

"Whatever you want to tell me is O.K."

She sat on the side of the bed. Zeb remembered times just like this when she had visited him as a child to talk to him, pray with him, nurse him when he was sick. She was always putting the rest of them first. He felt rage growing in him, not just against his father but at himself, too, for all the ways he had let her down.

"I woke up early that morning and lay there listening to him breathing," Jadine said, after a while. "His breath made a rasping sound that worried me. I tried to remember how long it had been since he'd been to the doctor for a checkup, I knew it had been a least a couple of years. You know how he was about going to the doctor. I decided to start working on him, trying to get him to go. He'd been drinking too much again. He was worried about the farm, as usual. Everything was stunted from the drought. It was like a plague. Tobacco all shriveled up and the corn only half its normal size. The ground was cracking open it was so dry. Chickens stopped laying eggs. And then Stella Coleman's boy, Earl, killed his brother Hinton with a sledge hammer. I prayed for them. Prayed for rain, too, but the rain didn't come. If it had, maybe things would have been different.

"Anyway, that morning I got out of bed and went into the kitchen. I found a bucket of fish on the back porch, most of them dead. I don't know where he caught them. I cleaned them in the sink and put them in the refrigerator. Then I got out some apples for a pie I was planning to bake. I started peeling them, shooing the flies away. I was already sweating. It was going to be another scorcher. The pie was for supper, a special occasion since Merle had invited his girlfriend, Theresa, home to eat. That was a first for him. He'd always been so shy about the girls he was seeing. I remember thinking, I'll put the linen tablecloth on and pick some flowers. I told myself to remind Lavis to spruce up, too. Merle's girlfriend is a Lassiter from Holden County. My daddy knew her daddy, Ervin. And her uncle Marion married my second cousin, Pam West. Marion and Pam live in Fayetteville and have two children. I remember thinking these were things I could mention to Theresa. And I was thinking that if she and Merle got married, the only one I'd have to worry about would be L.C."

Jadine had fallen silent. Realizing he had been holding his breath, Zeb exhaled. He felt dizzy, as if he had been spinning around with his eyes closed.

"Let's see, where was I? Standing at the sink peeling apples. I was remembering the way Lavis would come up and hold me from behind while I was standing at the sink or stove. That was back in the good times. I remembered how we used to go fishing on the Choctoosie, before you boys were born. I used to like to dangle my feet in the water, and Lavis would say, 'One of these days a big old bass is going to swim by and bite off your toes.'" Jadine was quiet awhile, and then she said, "I was thinking about those old memories so much I wasn't paying attention to what I was doing. I looked down and there was blood on my hand. I'd cut myself with the knife. I washed the cut under the faucet, thinking the heat was affecting my nerves. While I was doing that Lavis came in, wearing the same pants and shirt he'd been wearing the day before, even though I'd laid out clean clothes for him. 'Morning, honey,' I remember saying, 'I'll have breakfast ready soon.' He just stood at the screen, looking out the back door. 'I was going to fry that fish you caught,' I said, 'with some eggs and sliced tomatoes.' He still didn't answer. He pushed open the screen and went outside. The flies kept buzzing on the screen, and more of them were flying around the sink. I shooed them away with my hand, thinking I would have to buy some flypaper. My thumb wouldn't stop bleeding. I held it under the faucet again, and then I put salt on it so the blood would clot. I finished peeling and cutting the apples, then put them in the refrigerator. I got out the fish and started rolling them in flour. I was hoping a good, hot breakfast would get Lavis out of the mood he was in."

Jadine stopped talking again. He could hear her breathing, deep and slow. Finally she said, "I was putting the lard in the skillet when I heard the shotgun go off in the barn."

He could see her pushing open the screen and running down the steps, falling in the yard, then getting up and going on, crying his name as she ran, *Lavis, Lavis, Lavis*, her heart poisoned by the terrible knowledge that he was already beyond her reach.

Eight

When Zeb went off to Cedar Springs State University, his pockets jingling with money from old Elisha Beaumont, he was expecting his spirit to be uplifted and his mind challenged, not just by some of the South's most brilliant educators but also by the ancient masters: Plato, Socrates, Homer. He hoped to emerge from his study magically transformed by knowledge, a man with an understanding of history, a grasp of his age, and an insight into the heart of things. Although he had seen a few hippies when he visited Cedar Springs the past winter, he was surprised by what he saw the following summer. The campus and the town were filled with flower children: swirling on the sidewalks and grass, chanting, singing, playing musical instruments, tossing the *I Ching*, and staring into space in hallucinogenic wonder. Zeb walked through clouds of marijuana smoke, gawking at beads and beards and sandals and pierced ears and amulets and medallions and headbands and signs of the Zodiac and peace symbols and long, wild hair and half-naked bodies. In his white shirt, khaki trousers, and wing tips—standard attire back at Seaton High— he felt as incongruous as a space man wandering in a village of aborigines. Although the town lay only one hundred and sixty miles west of Seaton, in the heart of the state's rolling hill country, Zeb's first impression was that he had somehow entered a foreign nation.

As soon as he got settled into his dorm he called up Florine, who was attending a business college in Raleigh.

"Zeb?" she said. "Is this Zeb Dupree? Honey, are you still of the *world*?"

He took the bus to Raleigh on a balmy September afternoon after his last Friday class. Florine met him at the station. After covering his face with kisses she drove him around the city in her yellow Volkswagen, telling him about her horrible summer as a camp counselor. "The kids were all from filthy rich families, Zeb, and spoiled rotten. They were little monsters." Later, she took him to her cousin's apartment where they sat around drinking wine and listening to Florine's favorite singer, Neil Diamond. Florine's cousin had gone to the beach for the weekend, so they had the place to themselves. They made out on a fake leopard skin rug while Neil crooned. The preliminaries over, Zeb reclined on a pillow, ready to receive the same treatment he had received in the Andrew Jackson Hotel, but this time Florine was ready to go the distance. He trembled at first, and Florine had to offer some assistance. She was an experienced woman, having had an affair with her stepbrother when she was fourteen and a year later with a second cousin who was now a captain in the Air Force. She confessed these experiences afterwards while Zeb lay in sweet delirium on the rug. "But they mean nothing now," she murmured in his ear. "I want to give you everything."

"Why'd you make me wait so long when you weren't really a virgin?"

"Technically, I wasn't a virgin, but spiritually I was, because I was never in love those other times. Does that make sense?"

"No," Zeb said, "but I sure appreciate you giving me some, too."

At Cedar Springs Roseanne lost interest in her last high school boyfriend, Huis Yardley, and started dating a junior named Doug Rayford, whose father owned a string of fried chicken restaurants. The young prince of fried chicken owned both a silver blue Corvette and a cottage at Nags Head, where he and Roseanne often spent weekends.

"She's really in love this time," one of Roseanne's friends told Zeb.

Sometimes he would pass her on campus. In her monogrammed sweater, pleated skirt and Weejuns, she looked quaintly old-fashioned amid the students with electrified hair, beards, beads, and glazed eyes.

"Hey, Zeb," she would purr.

Her voice lingered like an exotic musk.

"Are there really communists up in Cedar Springs?" L.C. asked, when Zeb went home for the weekend.

"Yeah, there's all kinds of radicals up there."

"What do they do?"

"Make speeches, pass out pamphlets, try to get other people to think like them."

"If I saw a communist I'd bust him in the mouth," L.C. said.

"The other night on TV, we saw where a bunch of radish heads took over a college up North," Merle said.

"That's right," said L.C. "This one sucker was rared back in the dean's chair, feet up on the man's desk, answering the reporter's questions."

"They ought to drag them out by their hair," Lavis said, "and hang them up by their heels until they learn some manners."

"They were protesting the draft," Merle said.

"I'm going to register when I turn eighteen," L.C. said. "You ain't going to see me running off to Canada. I'm going to get myself an M-16 and run those yellow-bellied communists all the way back to China."

"Oh, hush, L.C.," Jadine said.

"Zeb, did you know there's niggers at Seaton High now?" Merle asked.

"Yeah. How many?"

"Fifty-some. It's that 'freedom-of-choice' plan."

"Ragus Hogan was one who come over," L.C. said. "You know he ain't a bad nigger."

"He's living with his grandmother," Merle said. "His old man ran off and left them. Then Mama Hogan took Plato and Eula up to D.C."

"First time I saw old Ragus walking down the sacred halls of Seaton High, I did a double take," L.C. said. "I said, 'Damn, Ragus, never thought I'd see you here, back when we were putting in 'bacca.'"

"What did he say?" Zeb asked.

"He just laughed and said he didn't expect to be there either."

"It's a sad day for Dixie when niggers can go to school with whites," Lavis said.

"They got a right to learn, same as everyone else," Jadine said. "By the way, Zeb, you haven't told us much about school. How have you been doing up there?"

"O.K."

"That all you're going to tell us?"

They were all looking at him.

He didn't tell them that he felt as lonesome and out-of-place at CSSU as Ragus Hogan must have felt at Seaton High; and he didn't tell them he had failed two calculus exams, and that the food in the cafeteria was bad enough to set off a prison riot. He told them about making an "A" on a history exam, about how he was acing his English themes, and spending most of his free time in the company of an exchange student from Paris, France named Fifi La Rue.

He had his mother and brothers spellbound. Lavis, however, got up and went outside.

A while later, Lavis returned to tell him Rainy Bowden was waiting to hear him play his fiddle.

"I left my fiddle at school," Zeb lied.

"Well come on outside and talk to him, then."

Zeb followed Lavis outside and down to the barn, where Rainy was leaning against his truck, his frog eyes shining in the light from the porch. He offered Zeb his hand. It felt like a piece of raw hog's liver. "Where's your fiddle, boy?"

"Back at school."

"You getting any pussy up there in Cedar Springs?"

"No, sir. Just studying."

When Rainy put a bottle in his hand, Zeb wasn't sure what to do. He glanced at Lavis for directions, but the old man's face was in shadow. What the hell, he thought, and he took a swallow of Rainy's whiskey. It was smooth and mellow. Rainy could afford to drink the best. Good years or bad years didn't change the way he lived, even though he sometimes outdid Lavis in poormouthing when a field of tobacco got torn up by hail or a drought ruined the harvest.

"What courses you taking, Zeb?" Lavis asked.

Zeb listed his courses: English, French, world history, calculus, biology, P. E.

Rainy held up his hand. "You see this hand?"

"Yes, sir."

"This is a working man's hand. You can study French and calculus up there at Cedar Springs until the cow jumps over the moon, but if you can't work, you ain't going nowhere. Now ain't that right, Lavis."

The old man's voice came low and sweet out of the shadows. "That's right."

"Now, where's your fiddle?"

"I don't want to play fiddle for you tonight, Mr. Bowden, and there's nothing you can tell me about work I don't already know."

Zeb went up to the house and sat down at the table, waiting for Lavis. Jadine, Merle, and L.C. were in the living room, watching TV.

Soon he heard Lavis's footsteps on the porch.

"Why in the hell did you act so ugly to Rainy?"

"Felt like it."

"Don't you sass me, boy. You ain't got so damned high and mighty that I can't still whip your ass."

"Rainy Bowden ain't nothing but a bag of hot air."

Lavis's neck muscles stood out like ropes. "You ain't no better than me."

"I didn't say I was. But at least I ain't Rainy's *nigger*."

He didn't try to fight Lavis back. When the others ran in, Zeb was on the floor, spitting blood, the old man still punching him.

"Lavis, stop it!" Jadine cried.

Lavis stormed outside, slamming the door behind him.

"What happened?" L.C. asked.

Zeb grinned up at Jadine, who was bending over him, trying to see if he had any teeth missing.

"Daddy don't love me no more," he said.

Dear Zeb, Jadine wrote, when he got back to school, *please forgive Lavis for hitting you, he hasn't been himself lately. He's been worried sick about money. We haven't made a decent profit on the farm for two years due to the lack of rain and we've been having trouble finding good help at harvest time. When the crops don't make money, you know how he blames himself. And he worries that Rainy will kick us off the place. He never would have blown up the way he did if he hadn't been so full of worry.*

Zeb wrote his mother to tell her Lavis could go suck eggs as far as he was concerned. *I've lost all respect for him,* he wrote. *And I don't care if I ever see him again.*

'Blessed are the merciful,' Jadine wrote back, 'for they shall receive mercy.' *I don't blame you for being angry, Zeb, but I hope you can forgive Lavis before summer, because we're really going to need your help with the tobacco.*

FAT CHANCE of me helping him this summer, Zeb wrote back. *I'm planning on staying in Cedar Springs.*

He knew Lavis didn't need his help nearly as much as his mama claimed. As for the old man's fear of getting kicked off the farm, Rainy had been dangling that sword over their heads so long, Zeb figured his father should be glad to leave, if only for the freedom it would have given him. But Lavis didn't look at it that way. Somehow Rainy's farm had become a replacement for the one he had lost, and he clung to it as if it was the last remaining hope of his otherwise doomed existence.

Jadine kept writing him, asking him to come home for the summer. In the spring he finally gave in and wrote to tell her yes, he would be there to help Lavis with the tobacco.

Florine took it hard when he told her he wanted to break up.

"Zeb Dupree, you're the most hateful, most deceitful man I've ever met. You led me on and took advantage of me—and I was practically a virgin."

"Please don't take it personal, Florine. I'm just not ready to go steady with one person now."

Although he enjoyed sleeping with her, Florine had been wearing on his nerves. Weekends when they didn't see each other, she called him to complain about the small miseries in her life—menstrual cramps, or a boil that had just popped open on her foot. He found most of their conversations inane and depressing.

A week after he broke up with her, Florine called to tell him about a dream she'd had about him. Old, broke, and lonely, he had been living under a bridge like a troll.

"That's what happens to people who are too emotionally crippled to love," she added.

Zeb's first day back home for the summer, Lavis drove him out Highway 11 to show him one of the new metal bulk barns Rainy had bought for one of his other farms. "How about this?" Lavis asked, as he showed Zeb the dials that controlled temperature and humidity. "And look here at these racks for the leaves. These bulk barns will cure twice as much as the old barns, in only seven days. Rainy Bowden is one smart man. These new barns will pay for themselves in three or four years, and after that it's pure profit."

Pure profit for Rainy, Zeb thought, as he kicked a can down into a ditch.

Lavis drove them down to Yancy's Bar, on Main Street across from the Seaton Post Office. They sat at the counter and ordered beers from Yancy. Lavis laughed and joked with the other men, ignoring Zeb, who was already regretting his decision to return to Seaton for the summer. Suddenly, Lavis put his arm around Zeb's shoulders. "Yancy, this boy has already finished his first year up at Cedar Springs State University," Lavis said loudly. "Looks like he's going to be the first Dupree to graduate from college."

Tears welled up in Zeb's eyes. He wiped them away with his fist.

Zeb, L.C., and Merle helped Lavis transplant the tobacco plants from the beds behind the barn to the rich lowland in the middle of the farm. They pulled off the "suckers," broke off the white blossoms when they appeared, and sprayed the plants with a chemical to kill the worms. They planted corn and soybeans, cultivating and spraying these crops, too, and helped Lavis feed the hogs. Some nights Zeb would come into the house too tired to do anything except fall on the couch and wait for his mama to call him to supper.

One night when Rainy came by to see Lavis, Zeb surprised everyone by appearing in the yard to play "Leather Britches," Rainy's favorite tune.

In July, Zeb read in the society section of *The Seaton Gazette* that Roseanne had gone to Greece as the guest of Mr. and

Mrs. Thomas Rayford of Columbia, South Carolina, and their son Douglas.

One Saturday night in August L.C. knocked Monk Masterson, a Seaton bad ass, through the plate glass window at Yancy's. When two Seaton cops, Homer Sessoms and Abner Caswell, came to arrest L.C., Homer said something to anger him, and in the ensuing fight, L.C. brought his handcuffed hands down on Homer's head, tearing off part of his ear. L.C. ended up in the county jail. The judge, Homer's cousin Buford, set bail at ten thousand dollars.

Lavis went to Rainy for help.

Rainy visited them Monday afternoon to tell Lavis and Jadine they didn't have anything to worry about. Rainy had spoken with the judge personally, and Rainy's lawyer was arranging for L.C. to be released from jail within an hour. Lavis was kissing Rainy's ass so much it made Zeb want to puke. ("Yes, sir, Rainy, we sure appreciate everything you're doing for us. We won't forget this, Rainy. Sure won't ever forget this.")

Rainy's lawyer got L.C. off with a fine and a suspended sentence. L.C. had to sell his car to pay the fine and Homer's hospital bill.

That fall, after the tobacco was sold, L.C. joined the Army and volunteered for Vietnam.

When he saw Roseanne in the student union, Zeb could tell something was wrong. Her hair had lost its luster, and there were dark circles beneath her eyes. He inquired about her trip to Greece, and she burst into tears. He led her to a nearby table, where he wiped her tears away with a napkin and listened to her story. Greece had indeed been wonderful but two weeks after they returned, Doug Rayford had thrown her over for another woman, an heiress. "I'm sorry to be carrying on like this," she said, "but we were secretly engaged."

"You'll find someone else," Zeb said, and he asked her out to dinner.

He took her to a basement restaurant off Jefferson Street. She needed to talk about her recent affair with Doug. Although Doug would one day own his father's fried chicken empire, he still wasn't satisfied; he wanted to be even richer than his father, and the heiress provided the perfect opportunity. Although plump and boring, she was to inherit ten million dollars on her twenty-first birthday.

Zeb kept filling her wine glass as he listened to her plight. By the end of dinner, Roseanne's cheeks were flushed, and she was smiling a little. Zeb paid the bill and walked her back to her dorm.

"Zeb," she said softly, her face dappled by moonlight, "I just know I'm going to be an old maid."

When he bent to kiss her she turned her face so that all he got was her cheek.

They began meeting for lunch that semester and for occasional dinners. Zeb made no attempt to seduce her; he knew his place. He was Good Old Zeb From Back Home. He could take her out to eat, listen to her problems, walk her to her dorm, at which time he was allowed a hug or a kiss on the cheek.

He figured he would take what he could get. He had already come a million miles since that autumn night when he had watched Jack Leland crown her Homecoming Queen, just another hick with a hard-on in the bleachers.

Sometimes he would go a couple of weeks without seeing her. When he would call her, she would be too busy to get together, but eager to tell him of a beach trip she had taken with her new boyfriend, Bernard, a third-year medical student. Once, Zeb ran into Roseanne and Bernard on campus. Bernard stood by, glowering, while Zeb and Roseanne talked. His presence at Roseanne's side made Zeb see he would need a good career if he was ever going to win her heart. But he couldn't see himself at medical school; he got sick just cutting up a frog in Biology 101.

His third year at Cedar Springs State, he decided to major in journalism, a trendy major on campus with a certain romantic allure. Even as he began his first news-writing course he was envisioning himself as a prize-winning reporter for *The New York Times*. He got a job on the student newspaper and began working on an in-depth story about the prisoners on death row at the state prison in Raleigh.

With photographs, his story took up two pages in the newspaper. Zeb considered his story to be the finest single accomplishment of his life. He had tried to tell the truth about the inmates, had struggled to reveal their humanity. Most of them had either taken someone out during an armed robbery, or else they had gone berserk and dispatched a sweetheart, friend, or family member. Although they frequently talked tough, they were all scared shitless, and who could blame them? Trapped like rats in their cells and knowing they would never see a river again or get a good sweet piece of ass.

The School of Journalism submitted his death row article to a national competition for student writers. The article won first place, with an award of one thousand dollars, which enabled Zeb to buy his first car, a used Triumph convertible. A story about the award appeared in *The Seaton Gazette,* along with his photograph.

In the meantime Roseanne had broken up with Bernard, and she was spending more and more time with Zeb. They went to the movies, to concerts, and out to eat. Spring arrived, and they began going on picnics. Zeb believed it was only a matter of time before she would be his. He waited for the right moment with patience and cunning.

And that moment occurred on a warm May night in a rented rowboat on Cedar Springs Lake. Roseanne unclothed was even more beautiful than he had imagined, and he entered her like a sinner at an old-time tent revival, who rises from his earthbound wickedness to walk toward the altar in a trance. Zeb's mind detached itself from his body and relished the scene from above: he saw his white bouncing buttocks, Roseanne's sweet face, and, just as he started to come, the bass that shot up out of the moonlit water, not five yards from the boat.

Exactly one year after Zeb saw the bass jump out of Cedar Springs Lake, he and Roseanne were married in Seaton's First Baptist Church, the Reverend Lamar officiating. A variety of social classes attended their wedding, including Mr. and Mrs. Woodrow Oliver, owners of Oliver's Funeral Home, and Mrs. Amos Yardley, wife of the man who now owned Lavis' homeplace. There were Wades, Adamses, and Gentrys, good Seaton families that went back generations. And all of Jadine's kin came up from Holden County: Oscar and Paola Deloatch were there,

83

and Darton Haysworth, the preacher at Gibbons Baptist, with his wife, Minnie. In the back pew Zeb noticed Daryl Jenks, Hank Thomas, and Amos Horton, men who hung out at Yancy's and drank with Lavis. Rainy Bowden showed up with his wife, "Lady Anne," a fragile, doll-like woman with vacant blue eyes. Rainy and his wife ignored Zeb, although he noticed them fussing over Roseanne at the reception. It was plain they resented him for getting above his raising. First he had gone up to Cedar Springs State University on a Beaumont Scholarship, then he had gotten written up in *The Gazette* for winning some kind of national journalism award, and now here he was marrying the Reverend Lamar's golden-haired daughter. The smart ass.

L.C. sent the bride and groom three dozen roses from Frankfort, Germany, where he was finishing his tour of duty in the Army, having survived a year in Vietnam.

At the reception Merle and Weasel Yow stood around gawking at women and looking like they would be more at home stealing chickens than wearing tuxes and sipping tangerine punch from crystal goblets. Merle was still living at home, working on the farm. Rainy Bowden had used his influence with the local draft board to get Merle an agricultural deferment. Weasel was home on leave from the Navy. Weasel's older brother Andy had died in the invasion of Cambodia. Zeb noticed Lavis and Daryl Jenks slipping out to Lavis's truck for nips from a bottle of whiskey. Later, Zeb saw Lavis with his arm around the reverend, who, at three hundred pounds, was nearly twice as big as he was. Lavis was bragging about Jadine's cooking and inviting the Reverend out to the house for dinner.

Roseanne's father had a sick look on his face, like that of a man who has just discovered a dead body in his bathtub.

Zeb and Roseanne were south of Miami, on their way to Key West, when she began stroking him between the legs.

"I'm going to pull off the road," he said.

"Find someplace private."

He turned off the highway and drove their rented, baby-blue Buick down a road past trailer parks, palm trees, orange groves, looking for a secluded spot. Roseanne was still stroking him. He couldn't find anything private, so he looked for something semi-private. He turned down a rutted roadbed that ran back into an orange grove. Farther down into the grove he could see some Haitians on ladders leaning against orange trees. He stopped the car and leaned over to kiss his new wife. "Baby, let's get into the back seat."

"But those Negroes can see us."

"No, they can't. They're busy working."

Roseanne looked doubtful. He kissed her neck, her shoulders. "I have to make love to you. Come on, they can't see us down in the back."

Leaving the engine running, they scrambled over the seat into the back.

"Zeb," Roseanne said, after a while.

"Uh huh."

"Oh, Zeb."

"Yes, baby."

"Oh, that's it. Just like that."

He was in such a state of bliss that he failed to notice the car had slipped out of gear and was heading deeper into the orange grove.

"We're rolling!" Roseanne cried.

"Yeah, baby."

"The fruit pickers can see us!" Roseanne was twisting and bucking like a net-snared jaguar. "They're looking!"

Her motions were exactly what it took for him to give up his seed.

He opened his eyes like Lazarus and saw orange trees rolling by, dark faces pinned to the leaves. Roseanne scrambled over to the front seat and grabbed the wheel. The tires spun in the sand as she tried to turn the car around. "Oh, shit, are we going to get stuck?"

"Rock it," he said, pulling on his pants. "Rock it back and forth."

The fruit pickers were climbing down from the ladders. They looked like they had O.D.'d on picking oranges years ago and been waiting for revenge. Roseanne got the car turned around and accelerated, shooting past orange trees to the road, while Zeb waved at the Haitians out the back window.

That night he lay again with Roseanne, their bodies entangled in a lovely communion of motion. Lavis and his misery were behind him now: the stink of the outhouse in July; the suppers of gravy, biscuits, and beans; the winter wind whistling down the hall while he bathed in the tub. Dead and gone. Say a prayer for the dead people who can't enjoy this. And for the celibate nuns and priests. Say a prayer for the pope, who Fergus Flynn claimed was the "anti-Christ." An unlucky choice, giving up the ecstasy of love for a wafer on the tongue, a basin of blessed water. Give me this day my sweet Roseanne.

Nine

The Confederate soldier stood at attention in the town square in Riverville, holding his musket across his chest, his granite eyes staring at the bridge. Zeb saw him as he drove across the bridge and turned right onto the road that ran along the edge of the Rocky River, slate-gray in the winter light. The river emptied into the Choctoosie, five miles northeast of Seaton. He turned into the parking lot of the Pier House restaurant and looked for Roseanne's car. He didn't see it. He was early, anyway. Waiting at the farm had been driving him crazy. That morning he had gone to a jewelry store in Seaton and bought Roseanne a gift, a silver necklace.

Inside the restaurant, a hostess showed him to a table overlooking the river. He told her he was meeting someone for lunch, and she left two menus. A waitress came to see if he wanted something to drink. Although he wanted a beer he ordered tea instead; he didn't want Roseanne to see him drinking. He wondered what he was going to say to her. He had to find out if she was still with Markham. Zeb could see now that Roseanne had been right when she had told him he shouldn't blame Markham for her decision to leave him; their marriage had started going downhill after Lavis's suicide. For weeks after the funeral, Zeb had walked around in a daze, unable to keep his mind on his work. The stories he wrote left his fingers like empty cans tossed into a junkyard. At night he was tormented by bizarre dreams. He became convinced he was somehow to blame for his father's death. By disproving Lavis's pessimistic vision of the world, hadn't he stripped the old man of his excuses for his own failure? Zeb's performance at work continued to deteriorate. He was drinking too much, coming in late, making careless mistakes in stories. The paper's general manager,

Tom Griming, suggested he take a week's vacation. Zeb took the week off, but when he returned, things weren't any better. Griming and Amos Suggs, the regional VP, gave him two warnings before they fired him. "We can't afford to compromise the success of this business because of your personal problems," Suggs had told him.

Zeb could see how neatly Lavis had turned the tables on him. He had left the old man's world behind in a big cloud of dust, trading it in for a beautiful wife, a white-collar profession, and a suburban home with an indoor toilet, but Lavis had destroyed it all with a single load of buckshot. It was clear the old man had had the last laugh.

As he sipped his tea he remembered reading once about a belief common among Australian bushmen. They believed in a mythical past called "dreamtime," when their ancestors had created the world. The ancestors later transformed themselves into certain trees, rocks, lakes, and hills, thereby investing the land itself with the bushmen's history. Lavis, too, believed that the best of himself lay in the past, in that homeplace on the river. But the best of Lavis lay somewhere else, Zeb thought, although he wasn't sure exactly where. He looked at the trees on the far side of the river and remembered his father carrying him through a moonlit field of corn.

He turned and saw Roseanne coming toward him. She wore a tight-fitting black dress that showed off her voluptuous curves and milky skin. A man and woman turned their heads to watch her go by.

He stood up, his legs trembling; although she gave him no encouragement, he greeted her with a warm hug. She was wearing a new perfume, and mingled with this fragrance was the odor of her period, a painful reminder of feminine fertility and their inability to conceive.

"You've done something different to your hair," he said.

"I got tired of it being long."

He helped her with her chair, and then put the gift on the table. "Merry Christmas."

"Thanks, I'll put it under the tree." She picked up the menu and began looking it over.

He couldn't take his eyes off her. He wanted the taste of her in his mouth, her scent on his skin. How could he have been so foolish as to let her slip away from him?

88

"When did you get to Seaton?" he asked.

"Last week."

"Did you drive?"

"I flew. Daddy met me at the airport."

"When are you going back?"

"I'm not sure. I'm waiting to hear from graduate school at Cedar Springs State. I've decided to get my MBA."

Zeb guessed her career move had something to do with Markham. I should have killed him when I had the chance, he thought. He stared at the menu, unable to concentrate on the selections.

When the waitress appeared to take their orders, Roseanne ordered clam chowder and a salad.

"And you, sir?"

"I'll have the same."

After the waitress left, he asked Roseanne why she wanted an advanced degree in business and not education.

"I'm not cut out to be a teacher, Zeb. There's real opportunity out there for women, in business and finance. I want to get in on the action."

"Markham going with you to Cedar Springs?"

"Actually, no."

"Is he history now?"

"I consider Brad to be one of my best friends."

"I can say one thing for old Brad, son of a bitch has some pretty teeth."

"What are you doing now, Zeb?"

"I'm painting condos."

"Really."

"Why didn't you answer my letters?"

"I thought it would be best if we didn't communicate for a while."

"All those months of not hearing from you, not knowing how to reach you—it's like you were dead. Not a day went by that I didn't think about you, didn't miss you."

"It hasn't been easy for me, either."

"You had old Brad to keep you entertained."

"I didn't come here to fight."

He put his hand on hers. "Roseanne, let's have dinner tonight. We don't have to talk about anything serious. We can drink some wine, watch the river roll by, have a few laughs. Like we used to. What do you say?"

"I'm going to be busy tonight."

"O.K. How about later, after Christmas?"

She moved her hand away. "No."

"Baby, what happened?"

"Things change."

"I didn't change."

"Yes, you did. Look at you: you've lost your confidence, your ambition."

"I know I let you down, but I never stopped loving you."

"I think you should know I'm divorcing you, Zeb."

He looked out at the river until he had gained control.

"Tell me something," he said. "Do you think we'll have a white Christmas this year?"

"What do you mean, you're going back to Cedar Springs?" Jadine asked, next morning.

"I just need to get out of Seaton a couple of nights, Mama. I'll be back by Christmas, if not before."

"It doesn't make sense for you to drive all the way here and then turn around and go back to Cedar Springs."

"It will only be for a couple of nights."

She followed him out to his truck. "Why do you let her do this to you? She isn't worthy of your love."

"I'll be back before Christmas, I promise." He kissed her and hugged her goodbye.

As he drove out to the road she stood in the driveway. He could see her reflection in the rearview mirror.

He kept seeing her all the way back to Cedar Springs.

Ten

Zeb lay in bed, waiting for Jadine to come in.

"Come on, Zeb, time to wake up and get ready for church."

"I've got a stomach ache, Mama."

"Must be all those pecans you ate last night."

He heard her calling L.C. and Merle. He pulled the sheet over his head.

But she came in again and yanked it down. "Come on, Zeb."

"I feel like I'm going to throw up."

"Where does it hurt?"

He put his hands on his abdomen. "Here."

"If your face froze like that you'd be a sight, wouldn't you?"

"I can't help it, Mama. It really hurts."

"All right. Stay in bed, then."

A while later, L.C. came in, wearing his blue suit and tie. "Faker."

Zeb pulled the sheet over his head.

Later, after they had gone into church, Lavis came into the room. "You ain't sick."

"Yes, I am."

"I'm going fishing."

"Can I go, Daddy?"

"A boy too sick for church is too sick to go fishing."

"Please, Daddy. I feel fine now."

"Sure you do."

"Please, Daddy. Let me go."

Lavis took his bag of tobacco out of his pocket and began rolling a cigarette.

"Come on," he said.

They were on the Choctoosie, not more than a hundred yards from Lavis's homeplace. The river was blue-green in the hazy light. They had caught three bass, a jack, and some perch. Lavis sat at the stern of the rowboat, sipping a hot beer, looking up at the ducks flying in V formation overhead.

Zeb was looking at the house on the river bank, where his father had spent his childhood.

"Daddy, tell me about that bear, Sam Crockett."

"Sam Crockett was a pure legend in this country. He usually hunted at night, but they could always recognize his tracks, because he was missing a toe on his back foot. He tore up many a cornfield in his time. Men came from as far away as Tennessee and Georgia to hunt him. They hunted him in the swamp and across three or four counties. Ain't no telling how many times Sam had been shot or how many dogs he'd killed. But after every battle he would always escape back to his kingdom in Wildcat Swamp, back to where no man had ever set foot. There was moccasins as thick as your leg in there—they could kill a man just by spitting poison into his eyes—and gators big around as tree trunks. Quicksand so deep it went halfway to China.

"Long about 1936 or '37, a famous bear hunter named Jack Slade came up from Georgia to kill Sam Crockett—swore he'd come out of the swamp with the old bear's hide. Slade was a giant of a man, six feet four and two hundred fifty pounds. Had seventy or eighty of the meanest bear dogs alive. The walls and floors of his house was covered with the skins of bears he'd killed. It was said he'd rather hunt bear than make love to a woman. Folks was laying bets on the outcome, and a lot of them was betting on Slade."

"Who'd you bet on?"

"Who do you think?"

"Jack Slade?"

"I bet what little money I had on Sam Crockett."

"Did you win?"

"Let me tell you the story. Now dozens of men begged Jack Slade to go on that hunt with him, but he only took one man, an

Injun who used to work for the Georgia prison system—they used him to track down escaped prisoners. That Injun could smell better than a bloodhound, and he could see in the dark. Once he got on a trail, it was like the Devil himself was after you.

"The day Jack Slade and the Injun went into the swamp after Sam Crockett, all the newspapers sent reporters to interview them and take pictures of them with Slade's dogs."

"Do you reckon they were scared?"

"Scared? About as scared as the north wind. It took them three days to hack their way back into the swamp where Sam lived, back to his kingdom. Then the dogs got his scent and off they went, howling like hounds from hell. Sam already knew they was there, though, and the old bear was ready for them. He started running around in a big circle, all through the most dangerous parts of the swamp, and seven or eight of Jack's dogs fell into quicksand, or got eaten by snakes and gators.

"Pretty soon Slade and the Injun figured out what the old bear was doing, leading the dogs through different trails to confuse them. So they got ropes on the dogs, and the Injun led the way. Now the gators and snakes just eased on back when that Injun come through, because he was just like death, see. Finally, Slade and the Injun got close enough to Sam Crockett to turn the dogs loose on him. And Lord, what a fight there was! Dogs hitting Sam from every direction, snarling and snapping, and he was batting them away, biting their necks, and grabbing them up and hugging them to death. He'd killed or crippled a dozen or more by the time Slade and the Indian got there. Slade raised his rifle and fired point-blank at the old bear."

Lavis was looking at the bobber on the river. "I believe I got a bite."

"Did he kill Sam Crockett, Daddy? Did Jack Slade kill Sam Crockett?"

"Just a minute." Lavis picked up his rod, reeled the line in a little, then set the fishing rod back on the edge of the boat. "The bullet didn't kill Sam Crockett. It just missed his heart. He was a mighty tough old bear, and he still had a trick or two to pull, because you see he was on his home territory, his kingdom. He skedaddled back into the swamp, into the briars and vines, with dogs clinging to him like leeches. He murdered up three or four more of them back in the briars, and there won't nothing Slade could do but grind his teeth and cuss.

"Slade and the Injun began hacking a trail through the swamp, chasing Sam farther back into his kingdom. The dogs caught up with him again near the Choctoosie River. When Slade and the Injun come up on the battle, the Injun got a shot at him this time. Sam hit the river and stayed under. When he come up for air, he was around a bend in the river, out of range of their bullets."

"Sam Crockett got away! Where'd he swim to?"

"He swam to an island on down the river. He dug in there, resting, eating fish and blackberries, to get his strength back. He crawled into the mud to cool the fever in his body and draw the poison out of his wounds."

"What about Jack Slade and the Injun?"

"Jack Slade was one mad gentleman. He was used to killing whatever he went after, see. But a third of his dogs was either crippled or dead, and the bear was still in his kingdom. Slade was beginning to understand that Sam Crockett won't no ordinary bear. Slade and the Injun left the swamp and come back to Seaton to buy more supplies and drop off the injured dogs. Then they had two big rafts made in town, for them and the dogs, and they went back down the river on the rafts.

"They hit the island at night, figuring they'd take Sam by surprise. They knew that's where he was. The darkness didn't slow them down any, because the Injun could see in the dark. But that Injun's night vision was his undoing."

Lavis was staring at the bobber again. "Looks like that nibbler is back." He picked up the rod and reel.

"Did they catch Sam by surprise?"

"No, but they caught him. Sam and the dogs was fighting down in a gully, and the Injun got right down there amongst them and stuck his rifle against Sam and pulled the trigger. The slug tore another hole in Sam. Before the Injun could fire again, Sam began to embrace him. Lord, that Indian commenced to hollering for Slade to help him, but Slade couldn't shoot down into the gully for fear of hitting the Injun. The Injun called out to the Great Spirit, and to six or seven lesser spirits to save him, but it didn't do him no good. Sam crushed the life right out of him and flung him aside like a rag doll.

"Jack had a lantern in one hand, his rifle in his other. He fired a shot at Sam, and then set the lantern down so he could slide the bolt back and get another round in the chamber. Sam Crockett charged up out of that gully and grabbed him, and down they went, with dogs swarming all over them. Jack was trying to get his bowie knife into Sam's heart, and Sam was trying to crush Slade the way he had killed the Injun. But Sam had lost a lot of his power by then, and maybe the dogs distracted him, too. He didn't kill Jack Slade; he just hugged him until Jack passed out and chewed up his right arm so it won't never any good again.

"Slade came to around daylight, and seen the buzzards circling, and the flies swarming over the dogs and the Injun. Slade figured Sam had crawled off to die, but he won't in no shape to look for the body. He'd lost a lot of blood, half of his ribs was broke or cracked, and his right arm was hanging useless at his side. It was all he could do to crawl back to the raft and go for help.

"Slade sent some men back to the island to bury the Injun and bring out the surviving dogs. They looked all over for Sam's body but couldn't find it."

"Did Jack Slade go back after Sam?"

"No. After Jack got out of the hospital, he went back to Georgia and started raising honeybees. He later became one of the biggest honey producers in the South."

"Did Sam Crockett live, Daddy?"

"Some say he did. Others claimed he crawled off to die of his wounds. Although the old bear was never seen again, I always liked to believe he survived that terrible fight and lived to die of old age, way back in his kingdom."

Lavis was looking at the old house on the bank.

"One thing's for certain: Jack Slade never took Sam's hide and made it into a rug."

Eleven

The hubcap was a silver streak above the field. He raised the shotgun to his shoulder, lined up the sight, and fired. The hubcap careened to the ground, knocked out of its trajectory by the number four shot. He broke open the shotgun, replacing the spent shells. He sat down on the running board of a milk truck and stared out at the field, the shotgun in his lap. It was Christmas Eve. Mama, Merle, and L.C. would just now be sitting down to supper. He took a drink of whiskey from the flask in his shoulder holster. He leaned his head back against the truck and put the muzzles of the shotgun under his chin. It would be easy to pull the trigger, he thought, his hand on the trigger guard. Just a light pressure and that would be it: no more Zeb. He stared up at the sky and contemplated what would happen. The number four shot would tear twin holes in his throat, mouth, sinuses, and frontal lobes. The holes, approximately two inches in diameter, would converge in his brain where the clumped shot would cause extensive damage before exiting through the top of his skull along with bits of brain, of bone, and a large quantity of blood. He put the shotgun back in his lap and reached for the flask again. He wondered what would happen to Henry if he pulled the trigger.

Snow fell like confetti in the moonlight, transforming the junked cars into white mounds.

The flask was empty. As he stumbled through the junkyard, around and around the cars, he could feel himself vanishing into the whiteness. His head was spinning. He fell on his face and got up, laughing. He fell again, striking something hard, and this time it was as if he were falling through a deep hole. When he stopped falling he opened his eyes and saw a figure coming toward him. It was his grandpa Joel.

He was floating in a warm, wet darkness. Then lights, voices.

"He be waking up, Mr. Cogswell."

A brown face hovered above: Jerome, one of the boys who worked for Tick.

"Welcome to the land of the living!" Tick boomed.

Zeb lay naked in a tub of warm water. His head ached all the way back to his neck. His fingers and toes felt like they were on fire. "What happened?"

"Life is what happened," Tick said. "You got yourself a second chance. You can sow your seed, boy. You can make whoopee."

"We found you in the snow," Jerome said. "You was turning blue."

"Your pup was out there in the road, hollering like he'd lost his best friend. Jerome heard him and went to see what was wrong. The pup took him right to you."

"You was passed out in the snow," Jerome said. "You pissed on yourself, too."

"We carried you into the house and put you in the bathtub to thaw you out," Tick said. "Hadn't have been for that pup of yours, you'd be froze solid by now."

There was a flutter of wings. The parrot landed on Tick's shoulder and peered down at Zeb. "Merry Christmas, asshole."

"Now you hush, Baby," said Tick. "Can't you see the man is feeling bad?"

"When I was young I wasted a lot of energy trying to measure pieces of time," Uriah Bozely had told Zeb one night, on the fire escape at the Tombs, "like it was cloth you bought at the store. But now I can see that trying to measure time is like swimming in the ocean and trying to count the drops of water that touch your body." Zeb hadn't quite understood what Uriah meant, but the longer he painted condos, the more he began to understand Uriah's philosophy of time. The job was so monotonous that winter that Zeb began to lose faith in the idea of measuring time, and then he began to comprehend the futility of the entire measuring process. All methods of measurement—ratios, formulas, equations, graphs, and probability curves—invariably left something out of the picture. As far as he could tell there was no way to measure all relative and tangential variables of a subject. His time spent painting condos was a case in point. Every weekday morning Duane would pick him up and drive him to the construction site east of town, where they would spend the day painting the interiors of the condos white. They would take a break around noon and eat Kentucky Fried or Mexican, then return to the condos, working until about five o'clock. At the end of the day he could calculate the hours he had spent working, but the resulting figure was meaningless, a mote in the immeasurable eye of space-time. The figure could not measure the value of his dreams and reveries or the joy he would have experienced doing something else—playing his fiddle, for example. Nor could it measure the weight of his sorrow or his boredom. It was only a bit of mathematical fluff whirling in the wind of humankind's puny efforts to make sense of the world.

Zeb's hands were callused, stained with white paint. Some days his life didn't seem to add up to much more than a pinch of lizard shit.

"You know the past is a funny thing," Duane said one morning on the way to work.

"How so?"

"For a year after Lisa left me, I'd wake up mornings and feel this empty space inside, like part of me was missing."

They were passing by the Mexican food joint, where they usually ate lunch. The thought of eating any more of that greasy, spicy food made Zeb feel slightly nauseated.

"I thought I'd put all that behind me, but this morning when I woke up, I had the same old feeling. Missed her so much I could hardly stand it." Duane swerved to avoid hitting a skinny dog that had run in front of the truck. "Love is a long row to hoe."

At night the bus shook and rattled in the wind, as if it were going down the highway toward some distant city where the

Spaghetti Brothers were to play. Zeb often wondered what had become of these musicians, and he even envied them a little. He told himself he hadn't given up on his dream of playing in a band. That plan, like everything else in his life, had simply been put on hold. On weekend nights he stayed up late watching horror movies on a small TV he had bought at a yard sale. Henry slept beside his bed and woke him up each morning by licking his face.

Nights he couldn't sleep he would go for long drives on the country roads around Cedar Springs. His nocturnal drives would always take him by the house of the girl with the gray, gold-specked eyes. The house was usually dark, the flatbed truck parked in the yard. On nights when a light was on, he would park his truck at the edge of the road and watch the house until the light went out.

One night he strolled up the driveway, intending to pay her a visit. But when he passed by her kitchen window he looked in and saw her bathing in a washtub in the middle of the room. Candles placed around the kitchen filled the room with a lemon-colored light that looked like mist through the frosted glass. He stood by the window watching her awhile before he returned to his truck.

Early in February he drove to Seaton. Jadine gave him hell, for not coming home at Christmas like he had promised, for not trying to find a decent job, and for not telling her what was going on. She was worried about his soul. "Son, you've got to turn your torment and confusion over to the good Lord. He will meet you at the point of your greatest need. Are you listening to me?"

"Yes, ma'am."

"You can hide from me, but you can't hide from Him. He reveals the deep and secret things. He knows what's in the darkness."

"Don't worry about me, Mama."

"I am worried about you. I want you to go to church with me in the morning."

Next morning they sat in the front row pew of the church and listened to a sermon on God's promise of eternal life. The preacher ended his sermon with a long prayer, and while Jadine held her son's hand in hers, Zeb remembered his old friend Andy Yow driving to school in his souped-up '57 Chevy with chrome side mufflers, racing tires and a horn that played a few bars of "Dixie." And on Halloween shaving his head and going as "Mr. Cue Ball." And that time they got drunk behind the tobacco barn. Andy, you were going to be a big star like Robert Mitchum in *Thunder Road*. You were going to own a Corvette and a yacht and have a different starlet every night. But in Vietnam a mortar caught you sleeping and blew your soul to kingdom come. At your memorial service the preacher said you gave your life for freedom, Andy. An "unsung hero" is what he called you. That afternoon a buffalo came down Main Street and people lined up on the sidewalks to watch it. The buffalo was old and dusty and looked like it had come a thousand miles. It kept bumping into parked cars. No one knew who it belonged to or where it had come from. Some boys ran after it, pelting it with rocks. We chased it out to Robert E. Lee Boulevard, past the new mall and Firestone Tire. The last I saw of it, Andy, the buffalo was running out onto the boulevard toward the county line—a blind, gaunt ghost of the American West.

PART II

Twelve

Daisies and violets appeared around the edge of the junkyard. Grass and weeds grew around the cars, concealing crushed, twisted metal. Butterflies swirled in the air overhead, and Henry, sleek and plump now, chased them through the junkyard, along with frogs, mice, squirrels, and rabbits. Evenings, the trees were full of whippoorwills.

When the weather turned hot, Tick organized the black boys who worked for him into "snake patrols." Arming them with tobacco sticks he sent them through the junkyard to poke under cars and into clumps of honeysuckle and piles of junk, with orders to kill any snakes they saw.

But the boys didn't find any snakes.

"You got to think about snakes before you can find them," Zeb overhead Tick telling two of the boys. "Just visualize snakes and you'll find them."

"Tick Cogswell is crazy if he thinks I'm going to be thinking about a snake," Jerome told Zeb later. "Only time I'm going to be studying a snake is if I lay eyes on him, and then all I'm going to be thinking is how fast I can be gone."

By the end of the week Tick's snake patrols had produced only one small black snake, which Tick himself found under a pile of tires behind the building at the entrance to the junkyard.

The flatbed truck was up on concrete blocks in the front yard, the tires gone. A turquoise 1959 Cadillac convertible was in the driveway. Zeb parked behind the Cadillac and walked around to the back porch, a roof supported by beams over a concrete slab.

There was a pile of firewood by the back door, along with an ax and a maul. Wind chimes hung from the rafters.

He could see her through the screen, sitting at the table. When he knocked on the wooden part of the screen, a chameleon that had been resting on the doorjamb glided up into the eaves.

She came to the screen. She was wearing a blue kimono. "Yes?"

"My name is Zeb. I gave you a ride last fall. Your truck had broken down. I was just passing by and thought I'd stop and say hello."

She stared at him a moment, then she opened the door. "Come in."

A potbellied stove stood on three legs in the center of the kitchen. To the left there was a sink, cabinets, a stove, and a window. There was a bedroom off to the right.

"I was fixing my seedbeds." She sat back down at the table. "Have a seat." There was a tray containing some boxes of earth on the table, and along with a small spade, some packages of seeds.

He sat down and watched her sprinkle seeds into her palm. Her hands were thin and red, the nails chewed down to the quick.

"Did you give up on the truck?" He wondered if she remembered him.

"I made it into a sculpture. I call it 'yard art.'"

"Where'd you get the Cadillac?"

"From my friend, Hannah. She got it in a settlement with her ex-husband."

"Nice."

"It gets me to work and back."

"Where do you work?"

"At the Midnight Special—know where that is?"

"Truck stop out on the bypass?"

She nodded, working with the seeds. "I'm working the day shift now which isn't so bad. My boss is a bitch, though, and sometimes the customers treat you like dirt."

"I've stopped by there a couple of times." It was all he could think of to say. He and Duane passed by the truck stop on the way to the condos each morning. He remembered there was a restaurant inside and a section that sold bullwhips, knives, postcards, and cowboy hats.

A peach-colored cat had appeared as if by magic in a pool of sunlight by the stove. It had a black mask, like a raccoon.

"Would you like some tea?"

"Sure."

She filled a teakettle with water and put it on the stove. A bill on the table was addressed to Jenny O'Brian.

"Where do you work, Zeb?"

"I'm painting condos right now." He thought maybe he should say that he had been a newspaper editor and that he was trying to find a job playing fiddle in a band. But instead he found himself telling her about getting thrown out of the Tombs because of Henry. "That fool who manages the rooms freaked out when he found out about Henry. He kept my deposit and threatened to call the cops if I didn't leave. I was looking for another place to live the day I gave you the ride."

The cat jumped into his lap and began purring.

"That's Sweet Pea in your lap. My name's Jenny."

"She feels full."

"She's pregnant." Jenny sprinkled some seeds into a container of soil, covering them up carefully with her fingers. "So where'd you end up living?"

"In a bus owned by Tick Cogswell."

"The junkyard man?"

"Right, you know him?"

"Anybody who drives a bomb knows Tick Cogswell."

The tea kettle whistled. When Jenny stood up the kimono fell open, revealing one of her small, shapely breasts. "I have orange spice and chamomile."

"Orange spice is fine."

She set the cup on the table, along with a spoon and a jar of honey. "Milk?"

"No, thanks."

The silence between them was lazy and comfortable. After Zeb finished the tea, he put the cat down and said he guessed he'd be going.

She followed him to the screen door. "Thanks for rescuing me last fall."

"Glad to do it."

"Come again," she called after him.

He drove off feeling somewhat disappointed. Since that day last fall when he had given her a ride home, he had thought of her as being exotic, mysterious. But she was just a waitress who lived in a shack and pissed in a hole in the ground. And, except for her eyes, she wasn't even that good-looking. Her face was too thin for one thing, and her hands were rough and raw. Still, she looked like she could use a good time. He decided to visit her again and ask her out. What the hell, he thought, she certainly seems available.

The next time he stopped by she was working with a hoe in a newly ploughed garden to the right of the driveway. She smiled and waved. "Hi, Zeb."

"Looks like you know someone with a tractor."

"My landlord. He charged me ten bucks." She was leaning on the hoe, her eyes shaded by a straw hat.

"I drove by last weekend, but your car was gone."

"I went to Nags Head. I'm working on an oil painting of a scene down there."

He picked up a handful of the red clay, crumbling it with his fingers. "I brought my fiddle. Want to hear a tune?"

"Love to."

He got his fiddle out of the truck and launched into "Arkansas Traveler." Jenny put down the hoe and danced around in the garden. The cat came out from under the shed to watch.

"You're really good," she said, after he finished. "Do you play in a band?"

"Not right now."

"I've got a guitar. Come on into the house and we'll play together."

They sat on a musty couch in her living room, trying to play some Fleetwood Mac songs Jenny knew. She sang in a husky, off-key voice. She had no sense of time, and the strings on her guitar were so old and sour it was impossible for Zeb to get them into tune. After a while he put his fiddle down. "What kind of painting were you working on at the beach?"

"It's a scene of the Hatteras Lighthouse, but it's not close to being finished. I've got some drawings I've done, though. Want to see them?"

"Sure."

While she went to get her drawings he looked around her living room. There was a fireplace, with a poster of John Lennon and Yoko Ono over the mantle. Several drawings hung on the wall in crude frames. The furniture looked salvaged.

She returned with her portfolio of artwork, which he examined with interest. There were scenes of fishing boats, harbors, lighthouses. Others were more striking: a chessboard with human faces on the figures, a hand hovering overhead; a clown studying a skull in its hands; some people in the water around a sinking ship, reaching toward some winged demons in the air.

"What's this one called?" he asked, holding the one of the people in the water.

"Salvation."

He held up another drawing, this one of a young girl bent over a stream, studying her reflection in the water.

"That one's called 'Leila.'"

"I like it." He gave her back the drawings. "I like them all."

"Want to play some more music?"

"No, I have to be going." He put his fiddle back in its case.

She walked with him out to his truck. "Thanks for stopping by."

"Would you like to go out sometime, maybe listen to a band?"

"Yes I would."

"What kind of music do you like?"

"Everything. Jazz, old-time, rock and roll."

"I'll see if I can find out what bands are playing."

"What's your number? If I think of something fun to do, I'll give you call."

He told her his number. "Want to write it down?"

"I can remember it."

He got into his truck. "I'll be seeing you."

"Wait." She ran into the house and returned with one of her drawings. She put it in his lap. It was "Leila."

"This is for you."

"I can't take this."

"Take it, please. I want you to have it."

She called him three nights later and invited him to attend a play with her. The play, *A Midsummer Night's Dream*, was to be presented by a touring Shakespearean company that weekend at a theater on campus.

He told her he would like to go.

"It takes about twenty-five minutes to get to the theater from my house," Jenny said. "That's allowing time to park. The play begins at eight. Why don't you come around seven?"

After he hung up, he recalled her shabby living room, the out-of-tune guitar, her scarred, red hands. He looked at her drawing, which he had taped to the wall above the couch, and wondered why he had thought about her so much all winter.

"Zeb, what was the name of that fairy who kept bewitching people?"

"Puck."

"And the king of the fairies, what was his name?"

"Oberon."

The Cadillac smelled faintly of roses. Before they had left for the play, Jenny had pinned a rose to her dress and another to Zeb's shirt.

They were outside of town now, passing Cedar Springs Lake on the left. The water shone like ice in the moonlight. He resisted the urge to dwell on the memory of the time he and Roseanne made love for the first time in the canoe. On the radio, a voice sang,

This ain't a love that's true,
but baby it'll have to do
until the real thing comes along.

She'll invite me into the house, he thought, and we'll drink some wine. Then we'll go into her bedroom. Everything will be easy and natural. She's been sleeping alone, too.

He pulled into her driveway and turned off the engine.

"Would you like to go look for four-leaf clovers?" she asked.

"In the dark?"

"I've got a flashlight."

"O.K."

"We can be 'merry wanderers of the night.'"

While she was in the house he relieved himself against her tire. He threw the rose into the garden.

She came out with the flashlight. "I haven't gone looking for four-leaf clovers once this year."

They went through her yard, down a path through the pines behind her house. Beyond the pines there was a pond. The brass-colored moon floated in the water like a lily. They walked along the edge of the pond, then up through more pines to a meadow.

She swept the ground with her light. "I found one!" She held it up for him to see. "Your turn."

"I've never found a four-leaf clover in my life."

"It's easy." She looked awhile, moving the light over the meadow. "Here's one. And, look, here's another."

"I must be blind."

"The trick is to look for four leaves. Don't even think about three-leaf clovers. They don't exist."

"They've all got three leaves."

She put two four-leaf clovers in his hand. "Here, hold these for luck."

But he couldn't find any.

She kissed his cheek and put more four-leaf clovers into his pocket. "Zeb, where's your rose?"

"Guess I lost it."

They walked back through the pines to the pond. Jenny wanted to go swimming.

"Go ahead. I'll keep a lookout for Indians."

"Unbutton my dress, will you?"

As he unbuttoned her dress, he could feel the heat of her body against his hand.

"Now the bra."

She slid her panties down her legs and waded into the water, her slender body pale and luminous in the light of the moon. She swam out to the center of the pond, dove, then broke the surface with a cry.

"Zeb, I just saw the fairy king!"

"What did he look like?"

"He wore shades and spats and a purple vest. He had on a fedora with a red feather in the band. And he was wearing a gold watch on his belt."

She laughed and dove again.

Zeb closed his eyes and saw the pond break open like the neatly cracked hull of a walnut, revealing the king of the fairies standing on the back of a giant tortoise.

"I have to tell you something," he said.

She sat up in her bed, her eyes wide in the candlelight. "Do you have VD?"

"No, I got a bad leg." He got up and took off his pants, then lay back down beside her.

She touched his leg, tracing a knotted scar with her fingers. "How'd it happen?"

"Tractor turned over on me."

"It must have really hurt."

"It did." He kissed her on the mouth, lightly running his fingers around her nipples. She was soon breathing fast, and her lips were hot against his.

But something was wrong; he couldn't get an erection.

He sat on the side of her bed, staring down at his mutinous member.

"This has never happened before."

"It's all right. It doesn't matter."

The hell it doesn't, he thought.

"I can help you." She touched him.

But he soon made her stop. "This is ridiculous. I don't know what's wrong with me."

"Maybe you're just tense." She lay with her head on his shoulder, her thigh against his.

"Are you frustrated?" he asked.

"No, I'm fine." She kissed his shoulder, and soon she was asleep.

But Zeb couldn't sleep. He wondered what was wrong. Had he been struck with some mysterious illness? It was a hell of a thing to happen after all these months of celibacy. He had felt plenty of desire for her when she was skinny-dipping in the pond. What in the hell was the problem?

He lay awake long after the candles had burned down to the wicks, feeling low-down and miserable.

Thirteen

"Jenny around?" Zeb asked the scowling woman behind the counter.

"She's busy. What for you?"

"Coffee."

The woman set the cup down so hard she spilled coffee on the counter. He picked up the cup and walked into the dining area of the truck stop, taking a seat in a booth by the front window. The tables were empty. A few customers sat in booths against the walls. Soon Jenny came through a door at the back, carrying a plate of food. She served the plate to a fat man in a cowboy hat. She looked skinny and pathetic in the uniform. Zeb had a sudden urge to leave, but it was too late; she had already seen him.

"Hi, Zeb. Not working today?"

"My partner was sick so we knocked off at noon."

"I'm glad you came in. Want something to eat?"

"I just came by to see if you'd like to go out Friday night."

"I'd love to."

"I thought we could get something to eat, maybe listen to some music."

"Jenny," the woman called from behind the counter, "you've got work to do."

"Who's she?"

"That's Ora Lee, my boss. I've got to go. She doesn't like the help to have visitors."

"O.K. Be seeing you."

"I'm working Friday but I'll be home by seven."

He finished the coffee and went up to the counter to pay Ora Lee.

"Great atmosphere," he said. "I'm going to tell all my friends about this place."

"Ora Lee is one of those sad people who have lost faith in life's possibilities," Jenny said.

They were sitting at one of the tables by the dance floor in the Saloon. The band, a rhythm and blues group from Atlanta, was taking a break.

"How long have you been working there?"

"Too long. I keep telling myself I'm not really a waitress, that the job is just a way to support my art. But after eight or ten hours of serving greasy food to hungry truckers, putting up with their rudeness and with Ora Lee's meanness, I go home and try to work, and my inspiration is on the ropes."

"Don't give up, Jenny."

"I couldn't even if I wanted to."

The band members returned to the stand and began playing a 1960's classic, "Midnight Hour."

"Zeb, let's dance."

"I'm not much of a dancer."

"Come on." She took his hand and pulled him out onto the dance floor.

He moved stiffly at first, but when the saxophonist went into a wild solo, the spirit of the music entered him like the Holy Ghost. He spun around and around, doing some fancy footwork. He guessed he was doing all right, for a crippled man.

When he pulled into her driveway, Jenny got a flashlight out of the glove compartment and ran to the woodshed to look at Sweat Pea's kittens.

"Oh, look, Zeb, I can see them!"

He knelt beside her and looked under the woodshed at the mewing kittens. The cat's eyes were phosphorescent in the beam from the flashlight.

"You'll have to find homes for them."

"I want to keep them all."

"I'm going to get a drink of water."

He went into the kitchen, got a glass down from the cupboard, and filled it with water from the faucet. He was tired, and his knee hurt from the dancing.

He was sitting at the table when Jenny came in, her face flushed.

"I counted three of them. I'm going to fix up a box for Sweet Pea and her babies in my bedroom." She drank a glass of water, too, looking out the window over the sink. "Zeb, I just saw a shooting star! I think it's an omen, especially coming right after Sweet Pea had her babies. When stars explode the dust will eventually form new stars, new life. All the atoms in our bodies were once part of stars."

"Do you mean we're just debris?"

"Some people, maybe. Listen, I'm going outside to look at them again. Want to come?"

"I'll wait here." He sat at the table, sipping the water. He pictured her thin face, her gray eyes specked with gold, her scarred, red hands. His knowledge of the utter hopelessness of her life gave him a sense of superiority. She was nothing like he had imagined back in the winter. He wondered if that was why he wanted to see her again, to be reminded of the illusion he had lost.

Later that night, after they had made love, Jenny lit a candle on a stand beside her bed. She lay in the crook of his arm, curling her fingers in the hairs on his chest, telling him about her life. She was from Cumalee, North Carolina, a small town on the coast. She'd had a difficult time as a teenager because she didn't get along with her stepfather.

"What happened to your father?" he asked.

"He died when I was nine. We were watching Mr. Rogers on TV, and my daddy started choking. He asked me to get Mama, and I ran to get her. When we came back in he was on the floor, turning blue. It was his heart. He was DOA."

"I'm sorry," Zeb said.

Jenny wiped tears from her eyes. "Me, too."

"What was he like?"

"He liked to laugh a lot and tell stories, but he was a wonderful listener. People were always telling my daddy their troubles. He should have been a social worker. He had a real estate business in town. I used to go down to his office every afternoon after school, and we'd go get ice cream. Mama and Gail, my sister, never knew we did that together. It was our secret. He probably did something with Gail that I didn't know about. He had a way of making everyone feel special. One of his many gifts.

"Anyway, two years after he died, Mama married Kelly Hickman, the football coach at Cumalee High. He owned some rental property in town, and everyone knew who he was, so I guess Mama figured she was getting a good deal. Kelly puts on a big act for everyone in public, but he has a vicious mean streak. We hated each other. My sister, Gail, was his favorite. She's an all-American beauty—a blue-eyed blonde with perfect features. She'd sashay around him and act cute, but I kept him at a distance. Also, I wouldn't do what he said, which really pissed him off. At first he'd just yell at me and threaten me. Then the beatings started. He'd beat me with switches, belts and, finally, his fists."

"What would your mother do?"

"Not much. Not then, anyway. Kelly was the big boss around our house. I ran away when I was fourteen. Hitchhiked to Georgia to stay with my father's sister, Angeline. I was on an exit ramp in North Georgia, and two men in a truck stopped to give me a ride. I shouldn't have gotten into that truck, but night was falling, and I was afraid to be standing on the highway after dark. They took me back into the woods and raped me. They beat me up and poured whiskey into my eyes. One of them had a knife, and he kept threatening to cut off my nipples. He was the worst. I finally got away from them after they fell asleep. I ran into the woods. But they woke up and came after me. I could hear them shouting; they said they were going to get their dogs and track me down. I kept running and running. Finally, it started to rain, and I figured I was safe, then, since the rain would wash my scent away. I spent the rest of the night in a tobacco barn.

"What little sleep I got was full of nightmares. I woke up exhausted, feeling so alone. I hurt all over, but worse than the pain was this sense that I had no value, that my life was a trashy useless thing, with no hope for beauty or love. It was the worst feeling I've ever had, and it came with the morning. I don't know how long I lay there before I decided to kill myself. I found a broken bottle, and I was getting ready to slash my throat with it when I heard this bird singing outside. It wasn't a pretty sound, just loud. I thought, you can't die with that racket going on, so I went outside to look for the bird. It was a catbird, way up in the top of a sycamore tree. I threw a rock at it, but it kept on singing. I threw another rock at him, and he hushed. I went back into the tobacco barn, picked up the broken bottle—and the catbird started in again. I went outside and threw rock after rock up into that tree, but I couldn't drive the bird away or get it to hush for long. I finally got so mad and frustrated I started crying. I cried and cried. That catbird was still singing when I left.

"I came to a farmhouse and asked the woman who answered the door for help. I didn't tell her about getting raped; I was afraid she'd call the police. I told her a dog chased me into the woods, and that I'd hurt myself trying to get away from it. I told her that my mother had died in childbirth and my father had been a lineman for the telephone company. I said he'd been killed a few weeks earlier by a downed line and that I was trying to get to my aunt's house in Augusta. The woman took me in, fed me, and cleaned me up. Two days later she and her husband drove me to the bus station and bought me a ticket to Augusta.

"When I got to Aunt Angeline's house I told her everything—about Kelly's beatings, about running away and getting raped. She was so sweet. She said I could stay with her as long as I wanted. She was a schoolteacher. I lived with her almost a month before Kelly and Mama found out where I was. They drove down and got me."

"Did you run away again?"

"No, after we got home, Mama actually stood up to Kelly and made him promise never to hit me again. She told him she'd leave him if he did. And he never did hit me again, either. But the rest of the time I lived there, we almost never spoke, which was fine with me. There was a wall of ice between us.

"After I graduated from high school, I came to Cedar Springs and worked my way through two years of graphic arts school. Gail graduated from East Carolina and married an accountant. She has two kids now, a brick house, and a new Buick. She even belongs to the country club."

"You see her much?"

"No, I haven't seen her since last year, but we write."

"How about Kelly? Ever patch things up with him?"

"I'm working on it. I don't want to walk around with all that anger inside. It's not healthy. And anyway, I just realized last year why I always hated Kelly so much."

"Why?"

"My psychologist called it 'displaced anger.' Kelly wasn't the actual person I was mad at."

"Who was that—yourself?"

"No. My father."

"Why were you mad at him?"

Jenny raised her head and looked at Zeb. Her eyes were wide and shining in the candlelight.

"For leaving me."

Fourteen

Zeb saw the notice on the bulletin board in the breezeway of the Saloon:

Fiddler needed for old-time band. 448-1377

"Duane, did you see this?"

"Saw it yesterday. I meant to tell you about it."

He dialed the number from the telephone in the breezeway and listened to a recording of a fiddle tune, then a voice: "This is Wade Rawlins. As you have probably already figured I'm not here right now. Please leave a message at the tone."

He left his name and number and joined Duane at the bar.

"That number belonged to Wade Rawlins, fiddler for Little Brown Jug."

"They need another fiddler?"

"I don't know. I got his answering machine."

Sloe Gin said, "Wade broke his finger playing softball. Doctor says he can't play for at least two months."

"They just need a temporary fiddler, then," Duane said.

"Everything is temporary," Sloe Gin said.

The next day, after he got back from Wade Rawlins's house, Zeb called Jenny on the phone to tell her the good news: that he had a job playing fiddle with Little Brown Jug.

"That's great news, Zeb."

"It's just for a while. Their regular fiddler broke his finger playing softball."

"Will you have to rehearse a lot?"

"No, most of their material is traditional."

"When's your first performance?"

"Next Saturday night at the Saloon. Can you come?"

"What a bummer. I'm scheduled to work Saturday night till midnight."

"Sorry to hear that."

"If you come over tomorrow night, I'll help you celebrate."

"O.K."

"Come around seven. I'll cook us dinner."

When he arrived at Jenny's house her kitchen smelled of spices and baked chicken. On the table there were two candles and a bottle of champagne in a bucket of ice. She served the chicken with fried okra, rice, homemade rolls, a salad, and the champagne. Sitting across from him at the table, her eyes sparkled in the candlelight.

"Jenny, this is a meal made in heaven. What kind of magic did you work on this chicken?"

"My secret."

"It's so good it's making my eyes roll back in my head." He rolled his eyes back for dramatic emphasis.

"Is your wife a good cook?"

"She was O.K."

"What does she look like?"

"She's about five six, weighs maybe two-thirty, and she's really into mud wrestling."

"Seriously—is she pretty?"

"Yes."

"I thought so. Why'd you break up?"

"I'm still trying to figure that out."

"Think you'll ever get married again?"

"No."

"I bet you will. You'll have lots of children, too. I can see them crawling into your lap when you come home from work."

"I can't picture it," Zeb said.

"You'd be a sweet old daddy."

After supper they took a blanket and walked back to the pond. There Jenny sat astride him, her hips gently undulating, while Zeb looked up at the fireflies. He saw Eula Hogan squatting in the pines, pissing. The magpie in the peach tree cocked its head, listening for Grandpa Joel's truck. A black racer slid across the floor in Lavis' old homeplace. Outside, a doe froze in the moonlight, listening to the distant baying of hounds. Oh, Jenny. Yes, yes, baby. This is God's own sweet pleasure, coming down into the heart like a rain of blossoms.

On his way out to the mailbox by the road, Zeb stopped by the junkyard office to pay Tick his rent. Tick was sitting at the counter, eating a hog's ear sandwich. On the counter there was a plate of fried hog's ears, a loaf of bread, and a bottle of hot sauce.

"Here's the rent," Zeb said. He put the money on the counter.

"Appreciate it. Won't you have a sandwich?"

"Thanks, but I ate already."

"What's going on?"

"I'm going to be playing with a band this Saturday night at the Saloon in Cedar Springs. I'd like to invite you to come by."

"I'll do that. What kind of music you all play?"

"Old-time, mostly."

"I like that kind of music. I'll bring Paulette, my new honey. She's a music lover."

"Got a new girlfriend, huh."

"Sure do. We been getting along like peaches and cream, too—except for the other night." Tick finished the sandwich, and wiped his mouth with the back of his hand. "We was back in the bedroom, and I was drilling for oil, don't you know. I had just struck that real fine sand when Baby commenced to hollering, 'Drive it deep, cowboy, drive it deep!' I got tickled then and started laughing, and that made Paulette mad. She got tightlegged on me. Took me ten minutes to talk her into letting me back in the saddle. I declare, Zeb, I'm going to put that bird in a stewpot one day."

"I'll believe that when I see it."

In the mailbox Zeb found an electric bill and a letter from Jadine. He read her letter while walking back to the bus:

118

Dear Zeb,

I have wonderful news! Merle and Theresa are getting married. They've set their wedding for Oct. 17, so mark that date on your calendar.

I am so happy for them. They get along great together. Theresa even goes hunting and fishing with him. She'll graduate from East Carolina at the end of summer school. She's in nursing. She's hoping she can get on at Memorial Hospital here.

L.C. has been seeing one girl a lot, but he won't tell me who she is. Abbie Johnson, who goes to our church, works as a hostess at the Pier House, and she told me he's been taking the same girl there every weekend. Abbie is going to try and find out who she is. L.C. can be so secretive. He's been that way ever since he came back from Vietnam.

I ran into Paola Deloatch at the PO last week, and she told me Oscar has cancer. They don't know how bad it is yet. He's going up to Duke Hospital for more tests. I hope you can see him when you're home.

Please come home soon. And let me hear from you. I worry about you so, Zeb. I know you've been hurt, but you can bounce back from this with God's help. Just put your trust in Him. (I don't know how I would get by without Him.)

Myron Sweetwater has been cultivating the field behind the house. It seems strange to have him working the land. I keep hearing the tractor out there and thinking it's Lavis.

Love,
Mama

He sat on the steps of the bus and read the letter again. It made him realize how estranged he had become from his family. He had no idea who L.C. was dating, and Merle was marrying a woman he had never met. I'm slipping away from them, he thought. I should do something.

But he felt numb, powerless to act.

"Zeb, do you realize how many people in the world have given up on their dreams?" Jenny asked.

"I hadn't thought about it," he said. They were eating supper in the Barbecue Shack.

"I'm talking about all the people who wake up every morning with nothing to look forward to, who go to jobs they despise and come home every night and sit in front of the television set, drinking themselves to sleep. Ora Lee is one, and Ron, one of the cooks at work, is another. I was talking to him yesterday about his marriage. He told me he and his wife haven't made love in over six months. And they hardly ever talk to one another. They have two kids and a trailer that's about to be repossessed. He misses the single life."

"Sounds like love slipped out the back door."

"I don't think so."

"Why not?"

"Because neither of them knew how to love. Ron said they were always holding back, trying to protect themselves. They'd both been hurt by earlier marriages that didn't work out."

"Why'd they get married again, then?"

"They were lonely. But they started out all wrong, tangled up in fear. I've loved like that, too. But I don't think it's the right way to love someone. You have to close your eyes and make the leap, trusting the air."

"Pass me the hush puppies, will you, Jenny?"

"The poet Rilke wrote, 'What is within, surrounds us.' Do you know what that means to me?"

"No."

"It means to change your life you have to work from within."

"What's the use in trying? We're just so much stardust. You said so yourself."

"We're more than that."

"How do you know?"

"Some things don't need explaining. They just are."

Through the cracked door of Jenny's outhouse, he could see her moving around in her bedroom. As he settled himself against the rough boards, it occurred to him that this was the first time he had used an outhouse since he had married Roseanne, and he realized he had made some kind of miserable circle in his life. He felt small and insignificant, like someone who had awakened up to find he has soiled himself in his own bed.

Fifteen

Saturday night for Zeb's first performance with Little Brown Jug, the Saloon was packed. He stood up on the stage, playing light runs on the fiddle, filling in the spaces, supporting the singers' voices. Once in a while, he would do a solo. The band was doing mostly fast, bouncy tunes, like "Jambalaya" and "Been All Around the World." People were up and dancing now. Shouting and stomping their feet. Zeb could not remember when he had been this happy.

They ended the first set with an original tune written by the bass player, Eli Corey. Eli, a fat man with a rust-colored beard, sang the lyrics:

> *Woke up this morning, there was demons in my bed.*
> *They were climbing up the walls*
> *and one was sitting on my head.*
> *They had fangs and whiskers*
> *and claws where their hands should be.*
> *Even saw demons when I turned on TV.*
>
> *Go away, demons, and don't bother me.*
> *You ain't no friends of mine*
> *and you ain't a-going to be.*
> *You know I have always tried to be fair*
> *but I ain't going to trust someone*
> *with snakes in his hair.*
>
> *If I had listened to what my mama said,*
> *I wouldn't have these old demons*

a-rooting in my bed.
I drunk a lot of whiskey, snorted cocaine, too.
Whatever brought me pleasure
that's the thing that I would do.

Go away, demons, and don't bother me.
You ain't no friends of mine
and you ain't a-going to be.
You know I have always tried to be fair
but I ain't going to trust someone
with snakes in his hair.

When the band took a break, Zeb saw Tick at the bar. He was hard to miss in his cowboy shirt and white Stetson. A big-breasted blonde in a purple pantsuit held on to his arm.

"Mighty fine music, Zeb," Tick said, shaking his hand. "This is Paulette."

The blonde planted a wet kiss on his ear. "I just love that blue-grass sound, honey. But I don't want to fool with no demons."

"Let's go out on the deck where it's cool," Zeb said.

He got a beer from Sloe Gin and they went out the back door behind the stage, to the deck outside.

"A blessing, Father Zeb!" Duane cried. He was leaning against the railing, flanked by a tall blonde and a short, curvaceous brunette.

"Give him a blessing," said the blonde. Zeb had seen her waiting tables at the Barbecue Shack. "He has a spiritual problem."

Zeb made the sign of the cross in the air over Duane's head.

"Bless you, my son. I hereby absolve you of the guilt arising from your pursuit of exotic perversions."

Duane bowed humbly while the women clapped, cheered.

"That's blasphemy, ain't it?" Paulette said.

"He's a priest," the blonde said. She held out her hand. "I'm Viv."

"Please to meet you, Viv. I'm Paulette Wilkins, and this handsome man here is my date, Mr. Francis Cogswell."

"They call me Tick," said Tick, tipping his hat.

"I'm Marla," the other woman said. She offered Paulette a toke on her joint.

122

"No thanks, honey. I'm scared of that stuff."

"You look a little bit like Dolly Parton," Marla said.

"I've been told that before." Paulette laughed and put her arm around Tick. "This here is Mr. Burt Reynolds."

"That couldn't be Burt," Viv said. "Burt Reynolds is a woman."

"Say that again and I'll scratch your eyes out," Marla said.

"It's true. Burt's real name is Gretchen Vittee and she hails from Bogalusa, Louisiana. All that body hair you see on Burt in her movies—the muscles, the deep voice—it's from hormone shots."

"Lord, you all are craaaazy," Paulette said. "Tick, you see the way people get when they smoke that wacky weed?"

"They're just having a little fun," Tick said.

When Zeb passed the joint to Viv, she smiled and said, "So what's it like being a priest?"

"Heavenly."

"I've always wanted to fuck a priest," Viv said.

It was past two AM, and Zeb, Marla, and Viv were in front of the Saloon laughing at Duane, who was up on the wooden deck doing an imitation of a rooster pouncing on a hen.

"Does he get this way often?" Marla asked.

"It's the paint fumes he breathes all day," Zeb said.

Eli Corey came outside, carrying his bass fiddle in its case. "Ye gods, what have we here? It's a gathering of the faithless and wicked."

"We've been purified by the fiddler," said Viv.

"Madam, this man can change his form at will. On full moon nights he becomes a bat, a scorpion, a snake."

"You're badly confused, sir," said Duane. "This is Father Zeb, the holy man."

"A father of darkness."

Marla held an imaginary microphone up to Eli, who had set his fiddle case down.

"Mr. Corey, if you're elected to office, what plans do you have for the country?"

"If elected I promise to prosecute the killers of our late beloved president, who was taken out by a consortium of international bankers and cuckolded husbands."

"What's your campaign slogan?"

"Rubbers for the retarded."

"That's our candidate!" cried Viv.

"Also: free love, free beer, and free pizza!"

Everyone cheered, applauded.

"Speaking of food," said Duane, "anyone want to ride down to Eddie's Diner for a burger?"

"I'm going to call it a night," Eli said.

"Good night, Mister Candidate," Marla called.

"Good night, lovely children."

The others got into Duane's truck, Zeb and Viv in the back, and rode down Whitmore Street to Eddie's Diner. On the way Viv slipped a pill into Zeb's hand.

"What's this?"

"Quaalude."

He washed it down with a swallow of beer.

"Give me a swallow, will you?" The wind was blowing her hair in her eyes.

He gave her the can, and she took a drink. Then she leaned over and kissed him on the mouth.

Eddie's Diner was full of late night celebrants; "A Hard Day's Night" was playing on the jukebox. Zeb asked Duane to order him a hamburger, then he went back to the john. On the wall over the urinal, he found:

A man ain't shit without a plan.

Someone had added a "t" to plan. Below were these additions:

What kind of plant, poison ivy?
Will a strawberry do?
That's a dingleberry, idiot.

He took out his pen and wrote,

I've got plenty of nerve
I just can't seem to feel a thing.

He used the urinal, then returned to the others, sliding into the booth beside Viv.

"Honest to God," Duane was saying, "it was a woman up top and a man down below. A 'he-she' is what I called it. Damned if I can figure out how he got those tits."

"The topic of this conversation is 'The weirdest thing I ever saw,'" Marla said to Zeb.

"Weirdest thing I ever saw was a cat," Viv said.

"A cat?" Duane said.

"That's right. I was up at Linville Falls, and a man and a woman came up with this cat on a leash. At first I thought it was a dog it was so fat. Its belly dragged the ground, and its face was big as a plate. Had a big gold tooth in its mouth. The man said it was twenty-four-karat gold. The couple had cameras around their necks, and I thought they had come up there to photograph the falls, but they just took pictures of that cat. The woman claimed it could understand everything you said. They had a special seat designed for it in their car."

"That's gross," Marla said.

"People eat cats overseas," Duane said.

"Duane, you're sick!" Marla took off his cap and hit him with it.

"Beat me," he said, winking at Zeb. "It gets me hot."

The waitress appeared with their food. While Zeb ate his hamburger, Viv's light, stroking motions on his thigh set off an electrical current that stirred the ganglia in his groin into a kinetic frenzy.

When he finished eating, she asked him to dance.

A Rolling Stones song, "Beast of Burden," was playing on the jukebox.

He stood up and she slid into his arms. Pressing his face into her neck he inhaled her aroma of sweat, soap, cigarettes. They slow danced between the booths and the counter, Viv rubbing her pelvis against him in a circular motion. He closed his eyes, imagining he was holding Roseanne. When he opened them the music had stopped and the bored drunks at the counter were watching him holding her ass.

"Walk me home, will you?" she asked.

"Where do you live?"

"Come on, I'll show you."

He left some money on the table. "I'm walking her home." His arms and legs felt like rubber.

"Good night, Viv," Marla called.

"Night, Marla."

Zeb and Viv walked down the alley behind Eddie's Diner and climbed the fire escape at the back of the Tombs. She had the first room on the left, with a window view of the alley and the pink neon hog over the Barbecue Shack.

"I used to live here," he said.

"It's a morgue, except the bodies can get up and walk around."

"How long you been living here?"

"Couple of weeks. I was renting a house with some other people, but it was sold. This was the best I could do on short notice." Viv rummaged behind the bed until she found a bottle of wine. She took a swallow and passed the bottle to Zeb.

"What do you do when you aren't working?" he asked.

"I'm a law student." She began taking off her blouse. "Help me unfasten my bra, will you?"

He helped her off with the bra. Then he took off his shoes and pants. "Don't you want to ask me how I got hurt?"

"Not really." Viv slid her shorts down her long, tanned legs. "I noticed you walked with a limp. Did you know that Jacob in the Bible walked with a limp? He was smote in the thigh while wrestling with an angel."

"I was wrestling with a tractor." Zeb took off his shirt and got into bed with her. Viv reached up to the switch on the wall and turned off the light.

"I knew a guy once who got his dick shot off in Vietnam," she said. He could feel her breath on his ear.

"Better to be shot through the heart," he said.

Sixteen

Sunday evening he drove over to Jenny's house.

"Come on in," she called, after he knocked on the screen.

She was in her bed, reading. The room was full of candles—on stands, on the dresser, on windowsills, all of them flickering in drafts.

"I missed you last night," he said.

"I'll bet."

"What's wrong?"

"Guess."

"Have a bad day at work?"

"I saw you."

"Saw me what?"

"Dancing with that slut. In Eddie's Diner."

He stared at the cat, nursing her kittens in a wooden box against the wall. He could hear them meowing.

"I saw Eli at the stoplight," Jenny said. "He told me you had gone down to the diner, so I went looking for you. I found you all right. You and Viv."

"Why didn't you join us?"

"You spent the night with her, didn't you?"

He stared at the nursing kittens. "Would it help if I said I'm sorry?"

"No."

He sighed, stood up. "I guess there isn't anything to say then, is there?"

"No," Jenny said. "There isn't."

"I feel like a dog, Duane," Zeb said, Monday morning on the way to work. "Jenny found out I spent the night with Viv."

127

"Here's a news flash, Zeb. Ain't no difference between you and a dog. A dog smells that poontang, and he goes after it. You're the same way, ain't you?"

"There's one big difference."

"What's that?"

"A dog don't feel guilty afterwards."

"Kind of makes you envious, don't it?"

Zeb looked at the pine trees passing by the window. He could feel a headache coming on.

Holding the hot gun across his thighs, Zeb sat with his back against the milk truck. The field was littered with hubcaps.

He heard footsteps and turned to see Tick.

"Practicing for dove season?"

"Just messing around. I owe you anything for the hubcaps?"

"Those in that pile ain't any good."

"I've been recycling them from the field."

Tick stood there, looking at the field. The sun was going down behind the trees.

"I just towed a brand new Ford in. Somebody hit it head on, crushed it like a tin can. I don't know why these fools on the highway drive the way they do."

Zeb broke open the shotgun and put two shells in the chamber.

"I lost my son in a wreck like that," Tick said. "He was home on leave from the Army. A drunk crossed the center line and hit him head on."

"When did that happen, Tick?"

"June fourth, nineteen seventy-one. He was driving a Ford, too."

"I'm sorry."

"I hate it when those kinds of wrecks come in."

"I reckon you do."

"He was a good boy, too. Wasn't a mean bone in his body."

Zeb stood up. "You want to take a shot at one of these hubcaps? I'll toss it for you."

"I don't have my glasses on, but what the hell."

Zeb went over to the pile of hubcaps. He picked one up and sailed it over the field. The shotgun boomed twice, echoing from the trees.

"Did I hit it?"

"I believe so," Zeb said, although Tick had missed both shots. He took the shotgun, reloaded it, and handed it back to Tick. "Ready for another?"

Tick stood there, his face bronze in the dying light, staring hopefully at the sky.

"I'm going to hit that booger this time."

"Pull in here, will you, Duane?" Zeb asked, Friday afternoon on the way home from work.

Duane turned into the parking lot of The Midnight Special. "What do you want here?"

"I want to see Jenny. I won't be long."

When he stepped through the front door, the floor and counter were littered with broken glass, spilled food, and coffee. A cook and a man in a cowboy hat were trying to separate Jenny and Ora Lee, who were struggling by the counter. The cook grabbed Jenny from behind and pinned her arms. The other man stood in front of Ora Lee, preventing her from hitting Jenny.

"You're fired, scumbag!" Ora Lee's face was purple.

"You can't fire me, you ugly bitch, because I just quit!"

As Jenny and the cook promenaded toward the door, a sugar bowl crashed against the wall. The man in the cowboy hat grabbed Ora Lee as she was reaching for a ketchup bottle.

"Did I come at a bad time?" Zeb asked.

"I got some hair." Jenny held up her hand to show him the strands.

"You best go on now, Jenny," the cook said.

Zeb and Jenny went out the door, leaving Ora Lee struggling with the man in the cowboy hat.

When they got around the corner of the building, Jenny began to cry. Zeb held her while she sobbed against his chest. Duane was looking at them from the truck, shaking his head. Zeb turned his palms up and shrugged, a picture of an innocent man.

"I thought about not seeing you any more," Jenny said that night. They were lying in her bed.

"What made you change your mind?"

"I didn't want to abandon you to that slut."

"I appreciate that."

"Was she good?"

"Would you believe I passed out before anything happened?"

"You expect me to believe that crock of shit?"

Zeb was silent.

"It's all right. I've been hurt before. I'm a big girl."

"Why were you and Ora Lee fighting?"

"I had an order up in the kitchen and she didn't think I was moving fast enough to get it, so she pushed me. One thing led to another."

"It was some fight."

"I'm glad it happened. Losing that job is an incentive for me to make some changes in my life. I need to get out of Cedar Springs for a while. I'm not doing the kind of artistic work I know I can do."

"Where do you want to go?"

"To the Outer Banks."

Jenny lit a cigarette and lay there looking at the ceiling. He could hear the kittens mewing in the box.

"You can come and see me if you want," she said.

"I'd like that."

"You won't come."

"Yes, I will."

"Promise?"

"Yes, I promise."

It didn't take her long to leave Cedar Springs once she had made up her mind to go. She sublet her house, found homes for the kittens, and had a yard sale to help finance the move. She even managed to sell the flatbed truck. The night before she was to leave, Zeb helped her pack her car with her clothes, cans of food, a tent, pots, pans, dishes, art supplies, and her drawings.

They said goodbye next morning in the driveway.

"You can help yourself to whatever you want in the garden while I'm gone."

"Thanks."

"I'll be seeing you." She kissed him. She was holding her cat.

"So long, Jenny."

He stood in her driveway watching the Cadillac until it rolled out of sight, then he walked up to the house and sat on the porch, staring at the garden. It was a neat, well-tended garden, with plants spaced evenly apart. He thought he should have told her he would miss her, since he didn't know when he would see her again.

A couple of days later, Zeb and Duane stopped by the Saloon after work. H.T. Slocum was at the bar.

"Good to see you, H. T.," Zeb said, shaking his hand. "Still at Lorenzo's?"

"I quit that turkey. I'm the kitchen manager at Darrel's now, out on the bypass. You'll have to stop by one night. We got some great ribs."

"I'll do that."

"What are you doing now?"

"Painting for Duane here." He introduced Duane and H. T.

"Me and Lorenzo had a falling-out over pay." H. T. held up his hand, showing a wedding band. "I got married in April, and we've got a little one on the way. That put everything into a different perspective."

"Congratulations, H. T. Let me buy you a beer."

"Fine. You can buy the next one."

"Here's a toast to dads," Zeb said.

"To dads." Zeb and H. T. clicked their mugs but Duane just sat there, staring down at his beer.

"Duane, you got something against dads?" Zeb asked.

"Not all dads. Just mine. When I was five years old he put on his hat and coat and said he was going out for a beer. He said, 'I'll be back in a while,' but the fucker never came back. In fact, I never saw him again."

"Did you ever hear from him?"

"No, but my brother saw him twelve years later in San Francisco. Roy, my brother, was in the Navy, and he was just getting off a boat from Japan. First thing he saw was our dad. Roy chased him along the docks a mile or more, but the old man gave him the slip."

"Maybe the guy he saw wasn't your father," H. T. said.

131

"It was him all right. Roy got so close to him he could smell his aftershave. The old man always wore English Leather."

"Now there's one slick individual," H. T. said.

"He was slick all right," Duane said. "He was the King of Slick."

"I knew a guy who was so slick he had trouble keeping his suit on," H. T. said. "His suit would just slide off his body and lay in a pile at his feet. Now he was the King of Slick." H. T. began laughing. "That dude was so slick he left a trail of slime wherever he went, like a snail."

"Who was that, H. T.?" Zeb asked.

H. T. was laughing so hard tears streamed out of his eyes.

"My daddy."

Zeb was walking down Jefferson Street one Saturday afternoon, and whom should he see but Roseanne? She was walking fast, her head held high, nostrils flared, her large, firm breasts jiggling beneath her Cedar Springs State T-shirt.

"Hello," she said.

"Hi." Zeb felt like his breath had gotten caught in his chest. They had stopped near the black ladies who sold flowers on the sidewalk. "What are you doing here?"

"I'm living here now." She said this as if she could hardly believe it. "I'm in graduate school."

"Where are you staying?"

She hesitated, then said, "In a duplex, on Emerson Avenue."

"You want to get together for lunch sometime?"

"Not now, Zeb."

"Just a suggestion."

"What are you doing?"

"I'm playing in a band. In fact, we're playing this Saturday night at the Back Street Bar on Whitmore. Why don't you come and hear us?"

"I've already made plans for that night."

"Maybe some other time then."

"I've got to go now. I really have a lot to do."

"Sure. So long."

"Bye."

He stood there watching her walk on down the sidewalk.

One of the flower ladies spoke to him. "Mister, want to buy her some flowers?"

"She doesn't want any flowers from me," he said.

Seventeen

Zeb sat on the couch in the bus, reading over the postcards he had received from Jenny. It was Saturday morning.

Dear Zeb, I'm living in a campground near Manteo and looking for a job. Last night I caught two sea trout from the pier. I rolled them in batter and fried them in a skillet on my camp stove. They were delicious. Sweet Pea got the heads and tails. This morning I heard about a restaurant that's hiring waitresses. I'm going to check it out today. Miss you. Jenny

Dear Zeb, My favorite times here are sunrises and sunsets. There are so many vivid colors here that you don't see much of inland—cerise and magenta and aqua. I think it has something to do with all the water. I have a job now. I'm a hostess at the King of the Sea, a restaurant in Kill Devil Hills. I start work tomorrow. I only have one dress and I'm flat broke. Guess I'll have to fake it. Jenny

Later that morning, when he went out to his mailbox, there was a letter from Jenny inside.

Dear Zeb,
I found a place to live. I'm sharing a cottage in Nags Head with a waitress who also works at the King of the Sea. Her parents own the cottage. I have my own room, but she says I'll have to sleep on the couch whenever her parents visit. That will be a drag, but the rent is cheap and the cottage beats the campground with the noise and bugs.

I'm working the 3-11 shift. I've been spending my free time painting and working on my sketches. I keep resisting enticements to go out and party. I want to keep my mind free of drugs and alcohol so I can work. I even quit smoking. It's been 17 days since I've had a cigarette.

Thanks for the letter. I'm glad you like playing with Little Brown Jug. I would love to be able to play a musical instrument or sing. (Did you ever hear that Gaelic proverb, "Everything shall perish save love and music"?)

This morning I went for a walk on the beach, and I saw a family of dolphins swimming close to shore. One of them raised right up out of the water and looked at me. I wish you could have seen them.

You're welcome to visit whenever you like. I'm enclosing a map to the cottage.

Jenny

He wanted to see her, but the next weekend was out of the question because he had a gig in Raleigh with the band. He wanted to go home, too, and see Mama, L.C., and Merle. He would have to take some time off from his job with Duane. But that would be all right. The condos they were working on were nearly finished, and they were ahead of the deadline. He didn't think Duane would mind if he took a couple of days off. He would drive over to Duane's house later and talk to him about it. Tonight the band was playing at a bar in Winston-Salem. He could leave for Seaton Sunday morning, spend a couple of days with his family, and then go on down to the Outer Banks to see Jenny.

Jadine was still at church when he got to Seaton. He stood in the doorway to the den, looking around the room—at the worn couch and chairs, the coffee table, the TV in front of the fireplace. On the mantel there were school photos of himself, L.C., and Merle, and an old photo of Lavis and Jadine, taken on their wedding day. A framed print of Jesus hung on the wall. In the center of the coffee table, on a doily, lay Jadine's Bible. There was a neat stack of magazines and tabloids at the end of the table. The top magazine had a marker in it. He opened the magazine and looked at the article's title: "Surviving the Loss of a Loved One."

He perused the lead story in one of the tabloids, about a doctor in Brazil who claimed to have successfully transplanted a baboon's heart into a baker. The story included a blurred photo of the baker in his hospital bed, surrounded by family members. Beneath the photo was this caption: *God has given me a second chance.*

He walked into the hallway and pulled aside the Oriental screen to look at the toilet and shower he'd had installed after Lavis's funeral. He remembered Rainy pulling him aside at Lavis's funeral—looking like a corpse himself with his bloated face and pop eyes—to tell him Jadine could continue living in the house. The toilet and shower had been Zeb's gift to her.

He walked on out to the front porch and watched Henry lift his leg against the front tire of Lavis's pickup. A pale blue haze hung over the land, making the corn and trees indistinct, like reflections in a stream. He sat on the steps and leaned his face against one of the posts that held up the roof. He had the sensation of being frozen in time, trapped in the past like a fly in an ice cube.

A car was coming down the driveway.

It was Mama, just getting home from church. He went down the steps and hugged her by her black Ford sedan.

"I didn't expect to see you, Zeb. Thought you'd given up on us."

"I've just been busy, Mama, playing with the band."

"When are you going to get a real job?"

"I'm hoping this might work into something full-time."

"I mean in journalism. That's what your education is in, isn't it?"

"I'm happy, Mama."

"I wish I could believe that." She sat on the steps and began petting Henry, who had been sniffing her shoes. "This past winter an old coon hound took up here. He was so old he looked human. Someone must have dropped him off on the road. He stayed close by the back porch. I was hoping he'd live to see summer, but he didn't make it."

"Mama, what's wrong with Daddy's truck?"

"I don't know. Merle tried to get it going last spring, and he finally gave up on it."

"We ought to get it running instead of letting it just sit there."

"We ought to do a lot of things." Jadine stood up and went into the house.

He petted Henry a minute, then went into the kitchen. His mama was talking on the telephone. "Merle, Zeb just got in. Can you come over for dinner tonight with Theresa? Good. We'll eat around seven."

She hung up and began dialing again.

"Who you calling now?" he asked.

"L.C."

"You don't have to go to all this trouble."

"It's about time you met your future sister-in-law."

"Get up, Dan!" Theresa cried. "Get up and bust him one."

"God, he's getting killed," said Merle.

Zeb sat with Merle and Theresa on the couch, watching the TV screen, where The Shadow stood over Big Dan McGrew, punching him back to the mat every time he tried to get up. The Shadow wore a black mask over his head.

Merle and Theresa had headed for the TV in the den after supper. L.C. had gone back to work.

"That blow is illegal!" Merle said. "It's a karate chop. It can drive his nose bone up into his brain and kill him."

"How you all can watch that mess is beyond me," Jadine said. She was sitting in the armchair, knitting a sweater.

The Shadow was sitting on Big Dan's chest, banging his head against the floor.

"It looks bad for the blond champion," the announcer said, as the camera zoomed in for a close-up of Big Dan's face. "How can one man stand all this punishment?"

Suddenly, Big Dan grabbed The Shadow by his mask and yanked him over backwards, clasping his thick body in the scissors.

"Big Dan has turned the tables on the masked man!" the announcer cried.

"Kill him, Dan!" Merle shouted.

After pinning The Shadow and winning the match, Big Dan strutted around the ring, flexing his muscles, shaking his blond ringlets at the cheering crowd. Their cheers turned to cries of warning as the Shadow slipped up behind him. Before Big Dan could turn around, the masked man hit him with a blackjack. Big Dan slumped to the floor.

The referee was gesturing wildly at The Shadow, as he stood over the fallen Big Dan. The crowd was going wild.

"He never should have turned his back on The Shadow," Merle said. They watched an instant replay of the scene.

"What did he hit him with?" Theresa asked.

"Looked like a blackjack," Merle said.

"He's an animal." Theresa looked at Zeb for confirmation. "Don't you think he's an animal?"

"I think he's the Devil," Zeb said.

Theresa frowned and looked back at the TV screen where two men in white uniforms were putting Big Dan onto a stretcher.

"Zeb? You awake?"

Jadine stood in the hallway, silhouetted by the light from the stairs.

"Yeah, Mama."

"I just brought this fan up for you." She plugged it into the wall and turned it on.

"That's a lot better. Thanks."

"I figured you were about to roast up here." She sat on the side of the bed. "I want you to be sure and see Oscar while you're here. He's been going up to Duke Hospital for treatments for his cancer. Paola said they don't know whether he's going to make it or not."

"I'll go see him tomorrow."

"What did you think of Theresa?"

"Seems liked a nice girl."

"She and Merle are together every minute when she's home from college. I'm so happy they found each other."

Zeb didn't say anything.

"Have you seen Roseanne up in Cedar Springs?"

"Saw her once."

"I heard she was going to school up there. She still have that boyfriend of hers?"

"It doesn't matter now. When I was home Christmas she told me she's going to get a divorce. She can do it after we've been separated a year."

"I'm sorry, honey. But you know you'll find someone else. Someone worthy of your love."

"I'm not looking for that."

"You don't have to be looking. It will just happen." Jadine touched Zeb's hand. "The Lord moves in his own way and time. We have to leave everything up to him."

After she left, Zeb lay there thinking about Roseanne. When she'd walked away from him on the sidewalk his heart had been jerking around like a man being electrocuted.

Why couldn't he just let her go?

After breakfast the next morning he drove down to see Oscar.

He found Oscar in his back yard, squatting by his beagles' pens. Oscar was gaunt and stooped now, his once splendid mustache sparse and streaked with gray. They sat in his truck and sipped whiskey from a bottle he had hidden under the seat. Zeb told him he was playing in a band.

"Glad to hear it, Zeb. Fiddler ain't going to make much money, but he's liable to have himself a fine old time."

"Feel like playing a tune?"

"Sure. Come on in the house."

Oscar had decorated the walls of his den with photographs of his old band, the Swamp Foxes. Although the band had broken up a few years before, for nearly twenty years it had been the most popular square dance band in three or four counties. He handed Zeb a fiddle. They tuned up and played "Muddy Roads," "Down Yonder," and "Sweet and Sassy." Zeb did some fancy things he'd learned—flourishes, riffs, and descending scales in triplets, just to show Oscar he hadn't been sitting still. Although he thought he had impressed his old fiddle teacher, Zeb realized he still couldn't play with Oscar's gentle touch, nor get quite the same lilt and sweetness from the melodies.

"Reckon you heard I got cancer," Oscar said, when they took a break.

"I heard," Zeb said softly.

"Doctor says I got a fifty-fifty chance." Oscar put his fiddle back in its case. "A man goes through life trying to satisfy all his desires—women, whiskey, money, power, whatever it is he wants.

I been that way most of my life, Zeb. Been lost in a dream." Oscar stared at Zeb so intently that Zeb shifted his gaze to the shelf containing the ribbons and awards Oscar had won in various fiddling contests. "But this here thing has made a believer out of me." Oscar closed his eyes and leaned his head back in the chair. "I've got to wipe the slate clean and start all over again, like a baby."

He opened his eyes and looked at Zeb. "You don't know what I mean, do you?"

Zeb shook his head.

"Did you forgive your daddy for what he done?"

"No."

"When you get to the place where you want to, you'll understand what I'm talking about."

Zeb picked up his fiddle. "Want to play some more, Oscar?"

But Oscar's bony hands remained folded in his lap.

"You'll see," he said.

When he got back to the farmhouse he saw L.C.'s truck parked in the yard. L.C. was sitting on the back steps. Jadine and the girl who worked at Lou's Diner were sitting in chairs on the porch.

L.C. had on jeans and a T-shirt with cut-off sleeves. High on his right bicep was the tattoo he had gotten in Saigon: a devil surrounded by flames with *Born to Raise Hell* tattooed underneath.

"Mama said you wanted to get the old Ford going," he said.

"Yeah, we ought to do that."

L.C. let his truck gate down and got a battery off the back. "Grab that tool box, will you?"

"L.C.," the girl called, "You all need some help?" She was wearing skintight jeans and a T-shirt with no bra underneath.

"This is man's work," L.C. said, winking at Zeb.

"A woman can do anything a man can do. And usually better."

"Maxine," Jadine said, "you want to come into the house and have some tea?"

Zeb and L.C. walked back to Lavis's truck.

"Sassy, ain't she?" L.C. said.

"How long you all been going out?"

"Few months. I ain't looking to get tied down."

"Don't look like she is, either."

"Let's get this truck running."

Zeb set the toolbox down and lifted the hood. L.C. set the battery down into the metal frame. "I borrowed the battery out of here back in the spring," L.C. said. "This is a replacement." While L.C. connected the cables, Zeb looked at the barn. Mud daubers swirled under the eaves. He looked back at the house and wondered how long it had taken Jadine to reach Lavis after she heard the shotgun.

"See if you can crank her," L.C. said.

He got into the truck and turned the key in the ignition. The engine turned over, but it wouldn't start.

"I'm going to prime it," L.C. said. "I got a can of gas in the truck."

A desiccated wasp lay next to a pack of Camels on the dash. He ran his finger in a circle around the wasp, leaving a trail in the dust. He opened the glove compartment and looked inside. He saw some wrenches, a stained map, a partial pack of Camels, some nuts and bolts, and a pocketknife with a broken blade.

Sweat trickled down his face. L.C. had raised the hood and was fooling with the carburetor.

"Crank her again, Zeb."

The engine fired this time. L.C. slammed the hood down and got in. Zeb put the truck in gear, let out the clutch, and drove across the yard to the driveway. He turned left onto the road that ran out to the tobacco barn, the truck bouncing and rattling in the ruts.

"She's running awful weak, L.C. Oil light is on, too."

"I just put in two quarts this morning. Seals must be busted."

He stopped in front of the tobacco barn, and L.C. got out to look at the engine. Zeb smelled hot, burning oil.

L.C. slammed the hood shut and got back in. "Must have happened while it was sitting up this winter."

"Is it worth fixing?"

"Not really."

Zeb drove back to the house. He could taste the burnt oil on his lips.

Jadine was waiting for them on the back porch.

"L.C., Merle wants to talk to you on the phone."

Zeb sat in the truck, staring through the cracked glass at the peach tree. Beyond, in the garden, stood the scarecrow Jadine had

fashioned out of straw and an old pair of pants and a shirt, one of
Lavis's slouch hats on its head. The scarecrow held both arms in
front of it, like a somnambulist, and appeared to be moving toward
the truck. Zeb closed his eyes, wiping sweat from his face. He
could hear the crickets and tree frogs raising hell outside the
pickup, parked now in the high weeds by the river, Lavis spinning
that old tale in his moonshine-drenched voice, a story Zeb had
heard so many times the words were imbedded in his heart like
shrapnel.

L.C. rapped on the truck.

"Merle has got his boss's cabin cruiser this afternoon. He's
going to pick us up at the dock at Slidell's beach."

Slidell's Beach was seven miles north of Seaton, on the Rocky
River. The beach lay at the end of a dirt road off Highway 11.
During the summer there was a dock and concession stand and a
lifeguard there. The owner, a farmer named Nick Slidell, charged
two dollars to spend the day.

On the way there L.C. stopped the truck too fast at a stoplight
and something slid out from under the seat, striking Maxine's foot.
She picked it up and said, "What's this thing for, L.C.?"

It was a machine pistol, with a long clip.

"Protection," L.C. said.

"That thing right there ain't nothing but a big mess of trouble,"
Maxine said, tapping the gun with her finger.

L.C. revved the engine, waiting for the light to change.

Zeb sat at the stern of the cabin cruiser, trailing his hand in the
water as she pulled away from the dock. He scooped up a handful
of water and rubbed it on his face. The boat was moving north,
toward the Choctoosie. The river shimmered in the sun, a pointil-
listic study in radiance. The wind sang in his ears. His face bathed
by sun and spray, he stared at the bikini-clad crotch of his future
sister-in-law and wondered what she was like in bed.

He stood up and got a beer from the cooler on deck. They were
sitting on cushion-covered seats connected to the side of the boat's
lower deck. He sat back down on the seat next to L.C., who was
rubbing suntan lotion on the back of Maxine's neck.

"Evil hasn't got a chance on a day like this," Zeb said, as the cold beer slid down his throat.

"Evil has got a better chance than you think," L.C. said.

The sun hung low over the river, streaking it fiery orange. The orange bled into copper, then mauve nearest the shore. Merle had dropped anchor, and the boat was rocking on the current. A song by Waylon Jennings was playing on the cassette player on the deck.

"Did you all read this story in *The Tattler,* about the guy with the baboon's heart?" Merle asked. His sunburned jaw bulged with a wad of Red Man tobacco. "Guy's ticker gave out, so the doctor transplanted a baboon's heart into him. He was going to die anyway so he didn't have anything to lose." Merle held up the tabloid, pointing to the blurred photo of the baker. "Here he is, right here."

"Where'd this happen?" asked Maxine.

"Brazil."

"Funny how those things always happen in some faraway place," Maxine said.

"He said he feels fine now except for one little thing," Merle said, winking at Zeb.

"What's that?" Theresa asked.

"He only wants to do it in a tree now."

"Baboons can do it on the ground," Maxine said.

"How do you know that?" L.C. asked.

"I been out with a few baboons."

"I'd feel weird walking around with a baboon's heart in my chest," Theresa said.

"Some people got the brains of a baboon," Maxine stood up and got a beer from the cooler.

When she walked by L.C. he pulled her down on his lap.

"Damned if this ain't the life right here." L.C. lifted Maxine's hair away from her ear and whispered something to her.

"Mr. Hines just keeps this boat to have a place to bring his women," Merle said. "I guess he figures his wife would have a harder time catching him on a boat."

"How long has he been letting you use it?" Zeb asked.

"This is the third time."

"Merle is his favorite," Theresa said.

"I'd like to have his money, I can tell you that," Merle said.

"You can get to where Mr. Hines is, Merle," Theresa said.

"We're going down below to take a nap." L.C. stood up, holding Maxine's hand. He winked at Zeb and turned up the music on the tape player, then went down the steps to the cabin.

Zeb leaned back and closed his eyes, listening to Waylon sing of hard living, lonesome nights.

He sat up suddenly and saw the abandoned house on the bank, swarming with ivy and honeysuckle, the windows like eyeless sockets.

Merle was looking at it, too.

"Daddy's dream house," Merle said. He spat a stream of tobacco juice over the gunwale.

That evening Zeb sat at the table with his head bowed, waiting for Jadine to finish praying.

". . . and bless all the children who will go to bed hungry tonight, bless the victims of war and the unfortunate ones who are living in darkness without benefit of the light of Jesus . . ."

The prayer over, he laid into the food: fried perch and bream they had caught that afternoon in the river, potato salad, slaw, hot biscuits and honey, sweet pickles and lemon meringue pie. While he ate he listened to the conversation around the table—gossip about who was running around on who at Finley's Poultry Processing Plant, a new shopping center that was going up on Robert E. Lee Boulevard, Andy Yow's little sister Irene, who had had a baby out of wedlock last month.

"I saw her on Main Street with it the other day," Merle said. "She won't a bit ashamed."

"She might as well hold her head high and love that baby," Jadine said.

"Possum Jenkins is the daddy, sure as I'm sitting here," Merle said.

"They used to come into the diner together," said Maxine. "Up until she started showing. After that, she came in alone."

"She must have wanted that baby bad to have it with no husband," Theresa said.

"I've got a whole lot more respect for Irene Yow than I do for Mr. and Mrs. Woodrow Oliver," L.C. said. "Remember that retarded girl they had?"

"They sent her away somewhere, didn't they?" Merle asked.

"She spent her whole life in some asylum up in Virginia. I wouldn't treat a dog the way they treated her."

Danny Oliver had told Zeb about his retarded sister Clara late one night after a dance at the Seaton Youth Center. Zeb had driven by the center and seen Danny throwing up in the parking lot and offered to drive him home. They had played football together before Zeb hurt his leg. Reeking of whiskey, Danny had rested his forehead on the dash of Lavis' truck and talked about Clara. Three months earlier her body had been shipped home from the Virginia sanitarium where she had spent her life. She was sixteen, a year younger than him, but he had never seen a photo of her, had never sent her so much as a postcard, hadn't even known for sure where she was. His parents' silence on the subject of his sister had been so relentless he had almost forgotten he even had a sister until the August morning her body arrived in the casket from Virginia. Danny had insisted Zeb drive them out to Memorial Gardens Cemetery so he could show him his sister's grave. He had no idea how she had died.

"That's how rich people like the Olivers handle kids they don't want," L.C. said.

"Not all rich people act that way," Jadine said.

"Pillars of the community," L.C. said.

"They'll have to make their peace with God." Jadine was staring at Zeb.

After supper Zeb helped the women clear the table, then took a pile of scraps out to Henry. He sat on the back porch, watching the pup eat. The sun had set, leaving a burgundy glow above the trees. The air was hot and still. Above the barn the moon was ringed with a yellow haze.

Soon the screen door squeaked and Merle came out. He sat down beside Zeb. "Looks like Myron Sweetwater has got himself a good corn crop this year."

"Myron and Rainy."

"That drought last year liked to have broke Rainy's heart."

It would have broken Lavis's heart, too, Zeb thought. Only his heart was already broken. I don't know how or when it happened: maybe when Ganton cheated him out of his share of the homeplace. Or maybe it broke slowly, over the years, cracking a little more every time he looked at himself in the mirror of Jadine's eyes.

"Feel like playing a tune?" Merle asked.

"Sure." He went into the house and got his fiddle. Theresa and Maxine were helping Jadine with the dishes. L.C. was on the couch in the den, watching a John Wayne western on TV.

He got his fiddle out of his room and went back out to the porch. Tuning the fiddle, he remembered the time he and Merle got into a fight in front of the barn; they'd been fighting over whose turn it was to look at a porn magazine they had bought from Andy Yow. Jadine had come out to separate them, and when she saw the magazine she broke a switch off the peach tree and flailed them like Jesus driving the moneylenders from the temple. Then she burned the magazine in the yard. Later, when she told Lavis about catching them with a "dirty magazine," all he had said was, "You boys should have shared that magazine instead of fighting over it."

"What do you want to hear, Merle?"

"Anything."

He began playing an Irish tune, "The Musical Priest." A cloud of fireflies appeared in the yard, as if evoked by the music. Soon Theresa came out and sat on the steps below Merle. She leaned back against him and he put his arms around her waist.

Jadine and Maxine came out and sat in the chairs.

Zeb finished "The Musical Priest" and began playing "Will the Circle Be Unbroken." This one's for you, Oscar, he thought, as he drew the bow across the strings.

Jadine sang the words in a low, sweet voice—all about how there was a better home waiting somewhere in the sky.

Eighteen

He woke up in Jenny's bed, sunlight in his eyes. He sat up and looked around the room of the cottage. She had decorated the walls with her sketches. On a table were some seashells, a piece of driftwood, paperback books, and, in a corner by a window, an easel holding her painting of the Hatteras Lighthouse. A face peered from the top window of the lighthouse. The sky was full of dark clouds.

He got up and put on his clothes. After a visit to the bathroom he went onto the back porch to let Henry out so he could relieve himself in the sand.

When he went back into the cottage, he saw a young woman in the kitchen, poking around in the refrigerator. Her hair was in curlers.

"I'm Zeb," he said. "Jenny's friend."

"Pleased to meet you, I'm sure."

"Where is Jenny?"

"On the beach. That your dog on the back porch?"

"Yeah."

"What happened to his eye."

"He was like that when I got him."

"Where'd you get him?"

"Found him in a trash can."

"Me and my brother used to throw kittens into those public mailboxes."

"What else did you do for laughs?"

Before she could answer he went back to the bedroom and put his trunks on underneath his pants. Then he went outside and crossed the road to the parking lot, following the path over the dunes to the sea. The Atlantic looked rough, with big swells rolling in. Except for the surfers, the few people in the water were sticking close to shore.

He walked down the beach until he saw Jenny. "Good morning," she called. Her hands were full of seashells.

"Morning."

"You were sleeping so peacefully when I woke up, I didn't have the heart to wake you."

"I met your roommate."

"Fran is depressed right now. She just got fired." Jenny pointed to a large beach towel on the sand. "Here's my towel."

Zeb took off his shirt and trousers and sat down beside her, curling his crippled leg underneath himself. She gave him a tube of suntan lotion. "Put this on, or you'll burn." He smeared the cream on his chest, face, arms, and legs. Jenny took the tube from him and he lay on his belly while she rubbed the lotion on his back. When she touched the back of his crippled leg, he flinched.

"Did I hurt you?"

"No," he said.

She lay down beside him.

"Don't you just love being here?"

"It's all right."

"It's more than all right."

"What made you pick the Outer Banks?"

"I have so many vivid memories of being here. Kelly and Mama used to rent a cottage here every summer. Beach houses are springing up like mushrooms now, but back then, the Outer Banks was more open and desolate. I loved everything about it—the marshes, the wildlife, even the storms. I've always felt so *alive* here.

"I remember how everyone used to worry when a big storm came in, but I'd get excited. Once when a really bad storm was coming, I slipped out of the cottage and ran down the beach. I hid behind the dunes and watched Mama and Gail looking for me. They wanted to leave for a safer place, but I didn't want to go. The sea was all silver and black. The sky was the color of wood smoke and all lit up with lightning. I ran down the beach, the wind pushing against me like a giant hand. And, Zeb, I saw this narrow strip of sand extending out into the sea. I took one step on it, testing it, then another, and another. I kept walking out into that stormy sea. It was so magical. I felt like I was touching the heart of the storm. From a distance I must have looked like I was walking on water. But the spell ended when a wave nearly washed me into the surf, and then I saw the sand bar collapsing in toward me. I turned and ran back toward the beach, knowing I'd drown if I went down into that violent sea. I thought I wasn't going to make it. But I did make it. When I looked back at the ocean, the sand bar was gone."

After breakfast, Jenny drove them out on the bypass to Jockey's Ridge, the big sand dunes in Nags Head that lay between the highway and the sound. They climbed to the top of the first dune and watched the hang gliders riding the air currents down to the flats below. Beyond the two highways and the cottages, the dark blue sea bled into the lighter blue of the sky. Jenny sat between his legs, her back to him, his arms encircling her waist.

"If you had one wish what would you wish for?" she asked. The wind was blowing grains of sand all around them.

"Wings, I guess."

"You'd like to fly?"

"Yeah. What would you wish for?"

"I'd wish I could make things happen by visualizing them."

"You could get a lot of wishes granted like that. Be like having a genie on call."

"I used to try to do that all the time, picture things in my mind to see if I could make them happen."

"Did you get any results?"

"Sometimes. I've gotten jobs that way, windfalls of money. Also, I've thought about certain people and had them pop up."

"That's interesting. What would you say your ratio of success to failure was?"

"I don't really know." Jenny picked up a handful of sand and let it sift down through her fingers, watching the grains scatter in the wind. "But it doesn't seem to work with love."

They returned to the cottage so Zeb could check on Henry again. Then they headed south on Highway 12 in Jenny's convertible, the top down. The sea was iridescent blue beyond the dune line.

"I need to see the lighthouse one more time," she said. "Before I can finish my painting."

"Why?"

"It has to do with something that's only felt, like the feel of smoke against your skin."

They were crossing the undulating bridge that spanned Oregon Inlet. Dazzling needles of light vibrated on the water below.

"That explanation isn't very clear, is it?" Jenny asked.

"No," Zeb said.

"I don't think I can explain it now."

Cape Hatteras Lighthouse loomed above them, its black and white spirals vivid against the clouds.

"It's the tallest lighthouse on the East Coast," Jenny said, as they went in.

She climbed the spiral stairs much faster than Zeb. He would find her on the seaward landings, gazing through the wire netting that covered the windows. They stood together at the top landing, watching the surfers ride the waves in. To the right, the shore curved around the sea in the shape of a crescent.

He stood behind her, his arms around her waist.

"I came here once with Daddy," she said. "Mama and Gail didn't want to climb all the way to the top. Daddy picked me up in his arms and carried me up the stairs. He asked me if I was scared, but I told him no, not as long as he was there. He carried me all the way up to the top and showed me this view. He said, "Look, Jenny, we're standing on top of the world.""

Zeb could feel her ribcage rising and falling beneath his hands. Her voice was echoing in the lighthouse. It seemed to come from all around him.

"For years after he died, I used to dream about this lighthouse. I'd be climbing the stairs, looking for him. I'd call out for him, but all I'd hear was the echo of my voice. I'd run up and down the stairs, looking for him. He was never there."

"What do you need to see here, to finish your painting?"

"I just need to look at it from different angles."

They went back down the stairs and walked down the beach. Zeb let Jenny walk ahead of him, and he waited while she studied the lighthouse, making sketches in a note pad.

"How's it going?" he asked.

"Fine. I think I've got it now."

On the way back to Nags Head, Jenny pulled off the road onto a parking area. "I want to show you something."

They got out of the car and walked down a path to the sea. To the right, on the beach, he saw a schooner, a ghost ship lying on its side, its mast broken.

"It's been buried in the sand," she said. "A storm uncovered it a while back."

"I wonder how old it is," Zeb said.

"Centuries." Jenny climbed up on the deck. "Isn't it wonderful? I can see down inside. It has a sandy floor."

"What do you see?"

"Blackbeard's head." She laughed and disappeared through a hole in the deck.

He climbed up onto the deck, too, and lowered himself into the schooner, down to the sand below. It smelled of brine and wet, rotting wood. Light streamed through missing planks in the hull.

Jenny was sitting in the sand, her back against the hull, her face and body neatly divided by light, shadow. "I want to make love," she said.

They undressed and lay down in the sand. The schooner was an echoing cave of sound. Jenny's face and throat turned scarlet. Sand clung to their skin. Her aroma of coconut oil and sweat mingled with the scents of brine, wet sand, decaying wood. She dug her nails into his back. Pressing his face into her neck, he could hear her crying in one ear, the sea in the other.

Afterwards, they lay in each other's arms.

"What are you looking for?" she asked. "True love?"

"I'm just trying to get by, one day at a time."

She raised herself up and looked at him. He could see the gold specks in her eyes. Her hair was full of sand. "Don't you ever wish you had someone riding shotgun?"

He smiled, picturing himself driving a stagecoach, with Jenny sitting beside him, holding his L.C. Smith. "I guess so."

"I'll be your shotgun rider, Zeb," Jenny said.

Nineteen

He played his last gig with Little Brown Jug at a wedding party in early August, on one of four sailboats anchored in an inlet near Wilmington. The sailboats were connected by gangplanks so the guests could walk back and forth. Two cabin cruisers ferried the wedding guests to the sailboats from a private dock.

During a break Zeb and Eli sat on deck chairs on one of the sailboats, sipping champagne and watching the groom pass out cigars on an adjoining vessel. The sea was bronze in the late after-noon sun.

"Where'd he get his money?" Zeb asked.

"He's up to his eyeballs in the drug trade," Eli said. "Wouldn't know it to look at him, would you?"

"No."

"He's descended from Southern bluebloods but the family's fortunes are about played out. Last two generations have been mostly drunks and slack-jawed idiots."

The groom took a bill from his wallet and lit a cigar with it. His guests whooped, applauded.

"You're looking at what may be the last hope of an entire bloodline," Eli said.

A willowy blond in a white dress walked by. Downing a glass of champagne, she tossed the glass into the sea and walked unsteadily across the gangplank to the next sailboat.

"Nice," said Eli, stroking his beard.

"You like my niece?" a woman asked. She had taken a seat in a nearby deck chair.

"I didn't know she was your niece, ma'am."

The woman, who was drinking a martini, had jet-black hair, and she was built every bit as good as the blonde.

"All she thinks about is water-skiing and boys. Last year it was fox hunting and boys. The year before, tennis and boys."

"She sounds very healthy."

"I hear she's a good lay." The woman smiled at Zeb. "Weddings bring out the animal in me."

At dusk, the wedding party moved to a bar near the dock, and from there to the home of the woman who had spoken to Zeb and Eli. She lived in an antebellum mansion near Wilmington.

In bed that night, the woman told Zeb that she and her husband, who was out of town on business, had an "open arrangement." Her bedroom overlooked a lush garden lit with floodlights with a fountain in the center.

"How long have you been a musician?" she asked.

"Since I was a kid. What do you do all day?"

"Nothing."

The woman was fascinated by his crippled leg. "Did you get hurt in Vietnam?"

"No."

"How'd it happen?"

"Listen, I can't go through with this."

"Why not?"

"There's someone else."

She laughed. "Your wife?"

"No, my girlfriend." He got up suddenly and began putting on his clothes.

"Looks like I'd learn," she said, reaching for a cigarette. "Every time I fool around with a musician, I always seem to draw a joker."

Standing in the breezeway of the Saloon, he slipped a coin into the pay phone and dialed the number on the business card in his hand. The card belonged to Willie Lee Hooker, lead singer for The Midnight Ramblers. Zeb had met Willie Lee in a bar in Raleigh a month earlier. He told Zeb he might need a fiddler and to give him a call when he got finished playing with Little Brown Jug.

Willie Lee was glad to hear from him.

"I sure do need a fiddler. Ever played electric?"

"No."

"Only thing different is the sound. What kind of arrangement you got with Little Brown Jug?"

"I just been sitting in for their regular fiddler. He hurt his hand, but he's back on the job as of this week."

"I see. We're going to be playing over in Cedar Springs this week. Know where the Casino is?"

"Bar out on the bypass?"

"That's the one. We'll be there Friday and Saturday night. Come on over and we'll talk."

After he hung up, Zeb looked at the business card again. Willie Lee's band was a country-rock group based in Raleigh, according to the card. The bar they would be playing in was a juke joint near the Midnight Special. He wondered how well the band was doing, and if they were any good. But even if the band was mediocre, at least he would be playing music instead of sitting around the bars, waiting for nothing to happen.

Friday night he arrived at the Casino as the band was cranking up to play. It was a four-piece band with a pedal steel. Willie Lee sported a white Stetson and a diamond earring. After kicking off the set with "Whiskey River," the band played a variety of songs, from fast tunes like "Ain't Living Long Like This" to slower songs like "Georgia on My Mind." Willie Lee had a clear, strong voice, with an impressive range, and he knew how to work a crowd. Both he and the band were better than Zeb expected.

He talked to Willie Lee at the bar after the band took a break.

"Appreciate you coming," Willie Lee said. "This here is Purdy Boyd, my bass player."

Zeb shook hands with Purdy, a thin young man with a protruding Adam's apple and glazed eyes.

"Let's grab a beer and go outside where we can talk," Willie Lee said.

Zeb followed them out to the band's van, parked behind the Casino. He and Willie Lee sat in the front, Purdy in the back.

"What did you think of the band?" Willie Lee asked.

"Tight and solid," Zeb said. "Fine vocals."

"That's what I like to hear. Electric is what's happening in music today, Zeb. Now I like Little Brown Jug fine, and they're the best at what they do. But let's be honest, nobody listens to that acoustic music anymore. Ain't no future in it. That's something me and the boys are interested in—the future. Ain't that right, Purdy?"

"That's right," said Purdy.

"We ain't just a goodtiming bar band. We got ambition." Willie Lee took a vial out of his pocket, sprayed his nostrils with cocaine, then passed the vial to Zeb. "Purdy, Zeb here is hot on the fiddle. I heard him play with Little Brown Jug one night at the Lion's Den in Raleigh."

"We need a fiddler," Purdy said. "Ain't no telling when we'll see Chombo again."

"Chombo is our regular fiddler," Willie Lee said. "He's in jail."

"What did he do?" Zeb passed the vial back to Willie Lee. The cocaine, like the music, was better than he'd expected.

"Purdy, tell Zeb what Chombo did."

"Got caught with his pants down."

"Now that there is an understatement. Chombo got into woman trouble, or, in this case, girl trouble. Preacher's daughter, wouldn't you know it. Won't but sixteen and already wild as a Texas twister. Chombo screwed her one night in the back of his car and never was the same again. Ain't that right, Purdy?"

"That pussy tore his head up," Purdy said.

"The little fox was slipping out her bedroom window to meet Chombo after her folks went to sleep. Her daddy got wind of it and called the sheriff. He caught Chombo and the preacher's daughter in a love embrace in the back of our boy's car. Found some pills in the glove compartment and some other illegal substances under the seat. To make a long story short, our fiddle player is in jail with a list of charges against him long as an elephant's dong. Ain't no telling when he'll draw a free breath again. How's that coke, Zeb?"

"Lovely."

"Glad to hear it. Here, have another toot."

Zeb felt as if a procession of street musicians was moving in his bloodstream, a ragtag band playing tambourines, guitars, bongos, sax.

"A musician needs a little pleasure now and then," Willie Lee said. "You know as well as I do that this music business is a fierce arena to be competing in. Most of us just scraping ass to get by."

Some conga dancers joined the procession. He could feel the beat: *coca-coca-ca. . . .*

"Being a musician ain't all sugar and bananas. But you know people see me up there in the spotlight, singing my heart out, and naturally they can't help but feel a little twinge of jealousy, because a musician is a romantic figure. But they don't see the hard times, the heartache, and the struggle, now do they?"

"I guess not," Zeb said.

"Course, they don't. Now Zeb, I want you to come in and play the next set with us. We got Chombo's fiddle on the stage. We'll just plug her into the amp, and you'll be ready to go."

After another hit of coke, Zeb went into the bar with Willie Lee and Purdy. Willie Lee introduced him to the other two band members, Snuffy Owens, the drummer, and Karl Rice, the pedal steel player. Purdy plugged Chombo's electric fiddle into an amp, and Zeb tuned it to Willie Lee's Stratocaster. The fiddle had a sharp, twanging sound, harder than an acoustic.

"Folks, we have a special guest appearing with us tonight," Willie said into the microphone. "On electric fiddle. I know you're going to love him. Ladies and gentlemen, please give Mr. Zeb Dupree a big welcome."

Zeb played along with the band as best as he could, filling in the spaces, not taking any chances. But on the bridge, Willie Lee told him to take it, and Zeb went into a spirited solo that generated whoops and applause.

The next day he found a letter from Jenny in his mailbox.

Dear Zeb,

Fran's parents came this past weekend, and I had to sleep on the couch. He's a shoe salesman with the imagination of a parking meter. She's frumpy, passive and bored. Both of them chain smokers. They spent the weekend getting drunk and watching TV. They went out just once—to play miniature golf. Why do they even own a beach cottage?

So much for the negative news. The good news is I SOLD MY FIRST DRAWING! A pen and ink of the harbor at Ocracoke. The day after you left I went down to the Seascape Gallery and showed the manager samples of my work. She took six drawings on consignment. This morning she called to tell me she'd sold my pen and ink for $35. I'm using my money to buy more supplies.

Last Saturday when Fran's parents were here, I was feeling so blue. I went for a walk on the beach, and a pelican flew down and walked beside me aways. There's so much magic in the world if we can only open up to it.
Jenny

He got out a pen and pad of paper, and wrote her a letter.

Dear Jenny,
I'm sitting on the front steps of the bus watching Henry stare at me with his lone, doleful eye. He is hoping for a dog biscuit. My head aches. My mouth tastes like I have been eating from a bucket of dust and ashes. Worst thing about getting high is the price you pay coming down.
I'm playing with a new band, a country-rock group, The Midnight Ramblers. Head rambler Willie Lee Hooker has big plans. He speaks of tours and concerts. He speaks of recording deals. I'm not sure how solid these plans are since last night's stories were spun on a cocaine loom. But it may be that I have to cut back on the time I spend helping Duane (not that I'll miss the work, which is barely fit for zombies).
Henry is winning the battle of the eyeballs. He has a distinct moral edge since I missed his supper last night.
Congratulations on the sale of your pen and ink.
Zeb

PS—The pelican was probably after food.

He told Duane about the new fiddling job Monday morning on the way to work.

"Looks like I'll have to cut back my hours, Duane. If you want to let me go and hire somebody else, I'll understand."

He had thought Duane might be angry but his friend just shrugged and said, "Let's wait and see how things work out. If you can survive life on the road, you're a better man than me."

Sunday morning, Willie Lee called to tell him he had arranged a seven-state tour for the band; they were leaving Tuesday morning.

"Why didn't you tell me before now?"

"I wanted to surprise you with the good news, and, anyway, I just put the deal together a few days ago. I did it with the help of an agent I've been working with. Listen, Zeb, we all stand to make beaucoup bucks."

"How much?"

"I ain't figured it out to the penny, but looks like it will be a right bodacious sum. Yes, sir, a right bodacious sum. Just put your faith in Willie Lee Hooker. I've got new strings on the electric fiddle, I've got the van tuned and lubricated; we're ready to go."

"Where will we be playing?"

"Georgia, Mississippi, Texas, among other places. And wherever we are, you can bet things will be hopping. I'm so happy I could crow like a rooster."

They left early Tuesday morning in the van, and played their first gig that night in a hotel ballroom in Columbia, South Carolina, for a convention of podiatrists. Later that night the agent who had booked the tour turned up in Willie Lee's motel room with some bad cocaine. The agent, who wore rattlesnake skin boots and a wide-brimmed Stetson, kept bragging about famous people he claimed he knew, like Dolly Parton and Don Gibson. He and Willie Lee strutted around the room like Harlem pimps, each one trying to outdo the other.

Zeb had to go outside for air.

From Columbia, the band went through Georgia, to North Florida, then across the Deep South, playing mostly in bars and nightclubs. The crowds were nearly always loud and drunk, and sometimes they were rude. After a week of being on the road with the band, the towns and cities began running together in Zeb's mind. To save money the band members slept three, and sometimes five, to a room. Things got so tense that Zeb began daydreaming about strangling Willie Lee. He would leave him hanging in the closet of some nameless motel room, his eyeballs bulging—a grim warning to America's half-assed dreamers who thought they could walk on air.

He called Jenny one night from the lobby of a bar the band was playing in.

"Zeb! Where are you?"

"Louisiana."

"I've been getting your postcards. You're really burning up the road, aren't you?"

"Willie Lee says this is the way to make it big."

"Have you been discovered yet?"

"Only by the bedbugs."

Jenny laughed. "Your last letter was hilarious."

"It was?"

"You said you were writing from a bathtub. In Biloxi."

"I don't remember much about that night. There was a big party going on. I took a pillow and blanket and went into the bathroom to sleep. I couldn't sleep, people kept coming in to use the john. So I wrote you the letter."

"You're so lucky to get to travel around the country. Mister Entertainment. All those women throwing themselves at you."

"Are you kidding? Do you know who comes to hear us? Zombies. From the heartland. According to the latest polls their main concerns are crime and unemployment. But those polls lie. Know what's really on their minds? Nothing. Absolutely nothing."

"Oh, come on, Zeb, it can't be that bad."

He could hear Willie Lee's Stratocaster cranking up in the bar. "I got to go, we're getting ready to play."

"Thanks for calling. I miss you."

"I miss you, too."

As Zeb walked into the bar, he heard Willie Lee say into the microphone, "Ladies and gentlemen, our fiddler is from the Louisiana bayou. He was raised on crawfish and gator meat. Learned to play fiddle before he even learned to talk."

During the more than three thousand miles Zeb traveled with The Midnight Ramblers he slept with a hooker, a barmaid, and a Mexican girl who spoke no English. He was drunk on all three occasions and later remembered very little of the experiences. The Mexican girl, who shared his bed in a motel room in San Antonio, Texas, was so thin her bones hurt his flesh. Afterwards, for some reason he never quite understood, Zeb began crying, and the girl held his head against her breasts and sang softly in Spanish.

When he woke up the next morning the Mexican girl was gone, along with his wallet and a Stetson Willie Lee had bought him in Dallas.

Twenty

In New Orleans Zeb saw a young girl with a club foot, selling flowers on the sidewalk. The girl, who wore a straw hat and a ragged blue dress, had solemn brown eyes and skin the color of honey. Her flowers had wilted in the heat. Zeb and Willie Lee were on their way to a restaurant near their hotel when they passed her. Zeb turned to look at her as he went by, and, a moment later, he asked Willie Lee to wait for him while he went back.

"How much are the flowers?" he asked.

"Twenty-five cents apiece." She smiled up at him.

"I'll take all of them." He gave her a twenty-dollar bill and went back down the sidewalk toward Willie Lee, who was shaking his head.

"That crippled child done snaked you out of your hard-earned money," Willie Lee said.

His first night back home from the tour, Zeb lay in bed thinking about the girl, as he had every night since he had seen her. Her face and eyes had glowed beneath the straw hat. It was a face eaten up with hope. "God bless you, sir," she had said, as he walked away with her wilted flowers.

Early the next morning Zeb drove into Cedar Springs for groceries and to pick up Henry from the kennel. When he got back to the bus, he gave Duane a call.

"Welcome home," Duane said. "How was life on the road?"

"It was an experience."

"I'll bet. I caught a mess of catfish in the river last night. Want me to bring you some over?"

"Sure. I'll cook us a supper."

He made a bowl of slaw and mixed up some batter for corn-bread. When Duane came over later, Zeb fried the catfish in an iron skillet. They ate on paper plates at the kitchen table.

Zeb described the tour, taking care to mention the problems—the drunken crowds, the tensions among the band members, the heavy use of alcohol and drugs, the bad food, and the psychic numbness he had begun to feel.

Still, when Duane asked him if he planned to go again, Zeb admitted that he would. "I don't blame you if you fire me."

"You can work part-time for a while. We'll see how things work out."

"Willie Lee says we're not due to go on the road again until October. But then I don't have a lot of faith in what he says."

"I met a hundred Willie Lee Hookers when I was on the road," Duane said. "He's just another aging dreamer with a bad liver and an ego the size of Texas."

"You said that right."

After supper, Duane got his Gibson out of the truck, and he and Zeb sat on chairs in the yard, playing music as the sun went down. They played a series of jigs, hornpipes, and reels. Soon Tick came back and sat on the steps, clapping his hands and patting his foot to the music. A bottle of whiskey appeared and was passed around. At twilight, the mosquitoes drove them into the bus. They spent the evening playing poker, drinking whiskey, smoking Tick's cigars, and listening to Zeb's record collection of old-time musicians, like Riley Puckett and the Skillet Lickers and Bill Monroe and the Bluegrass Boys.

Later, when Zeb and Tick went outside to relieve themselves, a silver sheen of moonlight covered the tree tops. They stood side by side, pissing into the pine straw.

"When I was a little feller I asked my daddy what the moon was made of," Tick said. "He said it was made of ice cream. I believed him, too. When I found out it wasn't, I went home and gave him hell for lying to me. Told him what I'd learned in school, that the moon come from a chunk that had broke off from the earth back during the dark ages of time."

"What did he say?"

"He said, 'What, you mean the moon ain't made of ice cream? Shit, my daddy must have lied to me, too."

Zeb and Tick laughed and, shaking themselves dry, they went back into the bus to play another round of poker.

That night Zeb dreamed Lavis came into his room and sat down in a chair by the bed, smoking a cigarette. The room was rich with the scent of curing tobacco.

"What in the hell do you think you're doing?" Lavis asked.

"Nothing."

"That's right. And that's all you'll ever be doing, too."

"Why'd you kill yourself?"

"To get outside of time."

"What about Mama? What about us?"

"Not my problem." Lavis flipped cigarette ashes into the cuff of his trousers. "I'm outside of time."

Zeb sprang off the bed, his hands encircling his father's throat, but Lavis disintegrated, leaving Zeb lying on the floor, rolling around in his father's ashes.

He woke up drenched with sweat and lay there listening to an owl calling in the woods behind the bus.

Henry woke him up, barking. Someone was knocking on the door of the bus. He put on his jeans and went to see who it was.

It was Jenny.

"Surprise!" she said. They hugged each other in the doorway. She looked young and tan in her white blouse and denim shorts. Her hair was in pigtails, tied with blue ribbons.

"Look." She picked up a paper bag at her feet. "Vegetables. For you." She came into the bus and looked around at the mess: empty bottles, ashtrays full of cigar butts, poker chips, and paper plates piled with fish bones. A squadron of flies circled.

"Had a poker game here last night," he said.

"I never would have guessed." Jenny set the bag on the table and went around the bus scooping up paper plates and dumping them into the trash can by the sink. Zeb emptied the ashtrays.

"Why don't you take the trash can outside and empty it," she said. "I'll get started on the dishes."

"You don't have to do this."

"Go on," she said. "Make yourself useful."

He took the trash can outside and emptied it in the garbage can at the end of the driveway. When he came back in, Jenny was washing the dishes.

"You back for a visit?"

"I'm back for good. The restaurant was a dead end scene. My boss kept promising me a raise, but he wouldn't come through. Fran's parents came down three weekends in a row, and she was bringing a different guy home every night. It all got to be too much."

He looked in the bag; it was full of tomatoes, peppers, and squash. "Where'd you get the vegetables?"

"From my garden. Hannah took care of it."

"She still living in your place?"

"No. She moved in with her boyfriend."

He helped her dry the dishes and put them away.

"Was the tour as bad as you said when you called?"

"It had its moments."

"For instance."

"I remember one time, about eight days into the trip, we were driving on a country road in South Alabama and Karl lost control of the van. We skidded down into a creek. No one was hurt, and the equipment was O.K. , but we were supposed to play that night in Brewton, and there we were in three feet of water, in the middle of nowhere, everyone really pissed off. Willie Lee had picked up this redhead in a honky tonk back in Georgia. She took off her clothes and jumped into the water. Everyone got into the water then and started splashing around. We had some food in a cooler. We built a fire on the creek bank, made a big pot of chili, and opened up some bottles of wine. That was about the best time I had on the trip."

"How'd you get the van out of the creek?"

"A farmer pulled us out with a tractor."

"This redhead, was she pretty?"

"I don't remember much about her. She was just hitching a ride to Biloxi."

"Only a slut would hitch a ride with five men in a van," Jenny said.

When the dishes were put away, she went out to her car and returned with her painting of the Hatteras Lighthouse. It had come a long way since he had last seen it. The lighthouse stood out vividly against the dark, gray storm clouds. Figures running on the beach enhanced the sense of an impending storm. The various hues of gray and brown and black added to the effect. It was an interesting scene of the lighthouse, and from an odd angle, but the crowning touch was the child's face in the lighthouse, which intensified the painting's surreal quality.

"It's beautiful, Jenny. Like something seen in a dream."

Jenny leaned her painting against the wall and sat beside him on the couch. "I didn't want to leave the Outer Banks until it was finished. It's the first big step I've taken in my goal of transforming my life from within."

"How can you do that with a painting?"

"It's hard to put into words."

He put his arm around her, and she rested her head against his shoulder, both of them still looking at the painting.

"It took me a long time to get it right."

"It was worth all your work."

"Thanks. You're the first person who's seen it." Jenny kissed him on the cheek. "I wanted you to be first."

"The waves look like they're moving," Zeb said.

Monday afternoon, when Duane dropped him off in front of the junkyard, Zeb saw a deputy sheriff's car parked by the office. He checked his mailbox and started walking to the bus. Soon the deputy's car pulled up beside him.

"You Zeb Dupree?"

"That's right."

"Got some papers for you."

It was a notice from the Sumner County Clerk of Court—to appear in court October 3rd if he wanted to contest Roseanne's divorce action against him.

Back at the bus he fed Henry; then he got his shotgun and several boxes of shells and walked through the junkyard to the pile of hubcaps. He stayed there firing at the spinning discs until it was too dark to see anything but the stars.

Twenty-one

In early September Jenny found a job photographing houses for a real estate company in Cedar Springs. She took the photographs in the morning and spent her afternoons at home working on her paintings and sketches. On Saturdays, she visited Zeb's bus to do his washing and ironing. She washed his clothes by hand in a washtub and hung them up on a line she had strung between two trees on either side of the yard. Each time she came she left fresh flowers in a vase on the table. She also darned his socks, sewed buttons on his shirt, and at least two evenings a week she would cook him a dinner. When he had to be out of town with the band, she took care of Henry for him.

"I saw that little gal down there hanging out your clothes the other day," Tick said, when Zeb visited him to pay the monthly rent. "She's a pure vein of gold, son. Better hang on to her."

"She'll do," Zeb said.

One Saturday afternoon he and Jenny got caught in a cloudburst by the creek behind the bus. Jenny's hands were full of lichen-covered bark and stones she had gathered by the creek. They ran up the path to the junkyard and climbed into an old Nash. Henry put his feet on the side of the car, whining. Zeb opened the door and Henry jumped into his lap. He set the dog down in the back seat. Jenny put her bark and stones on the dash.

"My landlord came to see me the other day," she said. "He's selling the house. He asked me if I wanted to buy it. I told him I'd love to buy it, but I was broke. Then I got a wild hair and went down to my bank to see if I could get a loan. Turned out the loan officer was George Griffin, my first official boyfriend back in Cumalee. We went steady for two months the summer after my sophomore year in high school. We broke up after his parents sent him to a private school in the fall. He was so handsome back then, with this long, black wavy hair. I couldn't understand why he even looked at me, I was so plain. Flat-chested, braces, skinny as a string bean."

"Maybe you had something he liked."

"I don't know what. All we did was hold hands and kiss—and share milkshakes at the drugstore. We drank out of the same straw."

"Did you get the loan?"

"No, we agreed I was a bad risk. Mostly, we just talked. He had really changed since high school. He'd gained weight and lost a lot of his hair. He had pictures of his wife and children on his desk. I wondered what she was like."

"She's probably overweight like him. I'll bet they have a gigantic TV in their bedroom."

"And a his-and-her towel rack."

"And a garbage disposal."

"And a waterbed."

Jenny laughed. "Just think, all of that could have been mine."

The rain was coming down harder now. They couldn't see out of the windows.

"Seriously," Jenny said, "do you ever want to have children?"

"No. Not now, anyway."

"Why not?"

"I'd probably just mess it up."

"I don't think you would," she said, but he could barely hear her for the rain.

The telephone woke him from a deep sleep. It was Jadine.

"Zeb, I want you to come home. L.C. is in jail."

"What for?"

"He shot up the town of Riverville."

"Anybody hurt?"

"I don't think so. I want you here, Zeb. I want you to talk to him."

"I'll be down first thing in the morning." He could hear Merle's voice in the background. "Put Merle on, Mama."

When Merle came on the line, Zeb asked, "What happened?"

"L.C. showed his ass is what happened. Sheriff Britt called Mama awhile ago and said they had him in jail over in Riverville. Said he went crazy and shot up the statue in the town square."

"He been acting strange lately?"

"Not that I could tell."

"Can you stay with her tonight?"

"Yeah, I'll stay with her."

"We're going to have to get L.C. a lawyer, Merle. I'll see if I can call one in the morning. You call Gil Henson and see if he'll sign L.C.'s bond."

"Will do."

"Put Mama back on, will you?"

His mother came back on the line. She was crying now. "L.C. has never been the same since he came back from that war."

Zeb stayed on the line until he got her calmed down. Then he sat at the card table in the bus, wondering what in the hell had gotten into L.C. It was clear that Mama expected him to come down there and straighten L.C. out, but Zeb couldn't even straighten out his own life. How could he possibly help his brother?

"L.C. wouldn't even talk to me," Jadine said next morning, when Zeb got to the farmhouse. "I tried to talk to him, Merle tried. He just lay on the bunk in the cell, staring at the ceiling."

"Did Merle call Gil?"

"Yes. Gil and the lawyer are over at the courthouse now. Gil told Merle he thought L.C. would be out this afternoon." Jadine put her head down on the table. "I don't know what to do."

He touched her, thinking she was crying. But she wasn't crying. She looked up at him and said, "I want you to talk to him, Zeb, you hear?"

He looked at her frayed sweater, her red hands, her swollen eyes. She spent forty-five hours a week working on the assembly line at Finley's. She came home after work to eat supper alone and then fall asleep with the TV on. It was church on Sundays, prayer meeting Wednesdays. Chicken guts and soap operas and Jesus the great redeemer. It wasn't the war that made L.C. crazy, Zeb thought. It was this: the poverty of the world.

And for the first time he thought he understood why Lavis had killed himself.

"I figured you'd show up," L.C. said. He was sitting in an armchair in his living room, bare-chested, wearing Army fatigues and paratrooper boots. Stevie Wonder was singing "Superstition" on his stereo.

Zeb turned the stereo down and sat on the couch next to the chair. "So how you been?"

"Mama called you, didn't she?"

"She was worried."

"Big shot. Mister Head of the Family." L.C. reached under the armchair and pulled out a flat, black pistol. He cocked it, aimed it at the wall, and squeezed the trigger. The hammer clicked. "Mister Big Shot."

"Cut out the tough guy shit, will you?" Zeb said. "I came here to help."

"College graduate." L.C. cocked the pistol again. "But you can't even hold down a job or keep your old lady at home. What's the matter, couldn't you satisfy her?"

Zeb lifted his hands, let them fall. "L.C.—"

L.C. pointed the gun at Zeb's chest and squeezed the trigger. *Click.*

"Mister Big Shot who ran away at Christmas."

"I'm not running now. And you know something else, L.C., you need your ass whipped."

"Who's going to do it?"

"Me."

"You ain't man enough."

"Would you like to step outside?"

L.C. put the gun down on the floor. Zeb stood up, opened the door, and stepped out onto the porch.

He hit L.C. as he was coming down the steps—a hard right jab in the nose. He followed it with a left to L.C.'s head that hurt his hand all the way up to his elbow.

L.C. sat in the flower bed, shaking his head. "Now you are going to die!"

He got up and charged, slamming his fists into Zeb's face. They traded punches awhile before Zeb went down on one knee, choking from a blow to his windpipe. The afternoon sun was behind L.C.'s face. Something slammed into his face and he went onto his back. L.C.'s face floated on the sun, a head on a sea of fire.

Gasping, he rolled over and got to his feet. Blood bubbled from his lips.

"Had enough, big brother?" L.C. asked.

Zeb straightened up with a punch that snapped L.C.'s head back. He hit L.C. again and again. He hit him so hard his shoulder hurt.

But L.C. didn't go down. He just staggered back, shook his head, and charged.

As Zeb stood there trading punches with L.C., he saw drops of blood fanning out in the air between them, and it occurred to him that he was letting Mama down.

Suddenly, he was on his hands and knees, his ears ringing, everything taking place in slow motion. He watched L.C. picking up a ball-peen hammer from the porch. He felt detached, as if he were watching the scene on TV. This feeling vanished when he got a good look at his brother's face as L.C. came toward him with the hammer.

"Go ahead and kill me, L.C.!" he cried. "Just like all those people you blew away in Vietnam!"

He covered his head with his arms, waiting for the blow that would smash his skull.

But the blow never came. When he looked up he saw L.C. sitting on the steps, his face in his hands.

Zeb stood up. His tongue found an empty place in his mouth where a tooth had been. He was looking around on the ground for the tooth when he saw three children standing in the yard, staring at him. He spat a mouthful of blood at them, and they scattered like quail.

He sat down on the steps, put his arms around his brother, and held him while he cried.

"Zeb, what happened to your face?" Jadine asked.

"I fell down. Listen, Mama, L.C. and I are going to be out late tonight. I came by to tell you everything is O.K."

"Sit down here and let me look at you."

"I'm O.K."

"Why'd you boys fight, son?"

"We just had a little misunderstanding. It's all cleared up now, I promise. L.C. just needs to cool out. He's been holding things inside too long. We're going to run Oscar's beagles tonight."

Jadine kept looking at him.

"Trust me, Mama. L.C.'s going to be all right. Everything's fine now."

"Let me make you boys some sandwiches."

"That's all right. We'll stop at Lou's and get something." He kissed her. "I have to go now, Mama. L.C. is over at Oscar's house, loading the dogs."

Jadine followed him to the door.

"Where will you be?"

"Daddy's old homeplace," he said.

He could see her standing at the kitchen sink, staring at her image in the glass. She would be thinking of a passage she had copied down from Corinthians: *Perfect love casteth out fear: because fear hath torment. He that feareth is not made perfect in love.* She would be seeing them out there on Lavis's old homeplace just as if she had second sight, would see them in that tangle of weeds, vines, and trees. Walking on the land that was Lavis's dream before Ganton robbed it from him. She would picture their faces in the starlight. *Perfect love casteth our fear* and *fear hath torment.* She would be thinking that she could see her father in each of them, Merle, too. He would talk to her but L.C. and Zeb just drew up inside of themselves like Lavis, and she couldn't reach them. She would remember Zeb telling her L.C. was going to be all right. But she would want to see L.C., want him to tell her the same thing. She would be thinking, *because fear hath torment and he that doeth good is of God; but he that doeth evil hath not seen God* and because what L.C. did with that gun yesterday had struck her to her knees, begging the good Lord to bless her with perfect love.

He parked his truck in the high weeds by the road and they sat there looking at the silhouette of the ruined house. The wind was blowing hard off the river. Oscar's dogs had been quiet on the ride out, but they were whining now. They wanted to hunt. L.C. went around to let them out of the cages. Zeb got the lantern, the cooler of beer, and the sandwiches out of the truck, and they walked back through the weeds toward the pines. The beagles fanned out, whining and sniffing the ground. No telling how long it had been since they had been hunting, with Oscar sick like he was. "Come on, Queenie," L.C. called. "Come on, Red. Jump that rabbit now."

At the edge of the trees one of the beagles jumped a rabbit, and they took after it, baying.

Zeb and L.C. sat in a clearing to eat the sandwiches they had bought at Lou's Diner and listen to the dogs. It hurt Zeb's jaw to chew.

"You look like hell, boy." L.C.'s right eye was swollen shut.

"So do you."

"Guess I fucked up."

Zeb popped the top on a beer and passed it to L.C. "You want to talk about it?"

L.C. stared at the lantern.

"I got a lot of things on my mind people don't even know about. I walk around, do my job, smile, make jokes, pass the time of day. But all the time I've got these—crazy thoughts, these memories. I used to think I could forget the war, but I can't. Everything keeps coming back."

L.C. cocked his head, listening. "They lost that rabbit."

"There's Queenie. She's got it again."

The beagles' frantic voices rose, fell, and rose again.

"Part of what keeps eating at me is that I'm still alive. I feel guilty for making it. So many of the guys in my company, Vince, Max, Lamont, got killed. And some of the others are really messed up now—they're missing arms, legs, eyes, parts of their faces. I survived all right, but sometimes when I get to thinking about those people the captain ordered us to kill, I get this feeling—it's like those people are still around, only invisible. I can't see them exactly, but I can feel their presence. That feeling will build up, and I'll do anything to get away from it—drink, raise hell. I'll be O.K. for days and then I'll have one of those dreams. I'll hear a knock on the door, go to answer it, and a bunch of them will be standing there, covered with dust and blood. Staring at me. Just staring at me.

"I'd had one of those dreams the night before I broke bad over in Riverville. It was still on my mind. I was lying in the Jackson Hotel with this woman I been seeing. She's married, so we get together on the sly. Lately, she's been dropping these hints about leaving her husband for me, she just wants me to give her the green light. But I don't want her to leave her husband. I like things the way they are. Anyway, she started giving me hell, making demands, telling me I owed her this and that. I was drunk and mad. She kept coming at me, her face all twisted, her fists clenched. And then she hit me. I looked at her, and I wanted to really hurt her. That urge kept getting stronger. I figured I'd better do something quick, so I stepped out of the room to cool off. But I couldn't cool off. This rage had just built up until I felt like I was about to explode. I got my Uzi out of the truck, along with a box of shells and a couple of spare clips, and started shooting at the first thing I saw—the Confederate statue. I gave that thing hell. Pretty soon, it looked like half the cops in the county were there, all of them aiming guns at me. Sheriff Britt was over by the hardware store, hiding behind his car. He hollered over to me, 'L.C., you put that gun down, you hear me?' I said, 'What you want me to do that for, Sheriff?' He said, 'Because we're going to have to shoot you if you don't, that's why.' I stood there a while longer, just to make them sweat some, and then I threw the Uzi down. They came out from behind their cars and took me to jail."

"Better the statue than the woman."

"Yeah. Listen, sounds like they lost that rabbit."

"No, there's Queenie."

"Sounds like Red."

"I can't tell for sure."

"Queenie's voice is huskier. That's Red all right." L.C. pointed to the cooler. "Pass me another beer, will you, Zeb?"

When Zeb handed L.C. the can of beer, he felt L.C.'s fingers touch his.

"I'm sorry I grabbed that hammer."

"What hammer?" Zeb said.

The wind was rising; they could hear thunder. Lightning flashed above the river.

172

"I guess we ought to round up the dogs and put them in the truck," Zeb said.

They got up and went through the trees, calling the dogs. They might have chased them over half the county if the rabbit hadn't run back their way. Zeb and L.C. caught the beagles as they were crossing an old roadbed and put them in the truck.

They were getting into the truck when Zeb got the idea of burning down the old man's homeplace.

"Everyone will think it got hit by lightning," he said. "That storm will be here before long, and the rain will keep the fire from spreading to the woods."

While L.C. held the lantern up in the living room, Zeb gathered up some old newspapers and magazines and put them in a cardboard box in the corner. Rain spattered his face from the hole in the roof. L.C. extinguished the lamp and poured the kerosene over the box of papers. Zeb lit a newspaper and dropped it into the box.

"Let's get out of here," he said.

They sat in the truck and watched the house, the flames flickering behind the windows.

"She'll be gone by morning," Zeb said.

But the house was still standing next morning when they returned: ugly, rain-rotted, black. Part of the wall had burned, that was all. Zeb could smell the sour stench of their failure.

He kicked a board out of the way. "Rain put it out."

"Rain and wind," said L.C.

They stood on the porch, looking at the river.

"Let's go get a beer," L.C. said.

PART III

Twenty-two

It was Friday night, and Zeb and Jenny were at The Skyline Drive-In, watching a western. Zeb had been working hard all week with Duane, and he was hoping he and Jenny could have a good time. But she'd been irritable and withdrawn lately, and tonight wasn't any different. After the movie started, she asked him to get her some lemonade at the concession stand. He went to the stand, stood in line, and got her the drink. When he came back, he got into the car a little too fast, spilling some of the lemonade on her.

"Be careful, will you?"

"Jenny, what's wrong?"

"Why does something have to be wrong?"

"You're acting strange."

"I'm *pregnant*."

"Jesus. Are you sure?"

"Yes, I'm sure."

He hung the microphone on the stand, then rolled the window up. His chest felt hot and tight, and there was a sour taste in his mouth.

"It happened on the Outer Banks," she said, after a while. "In that ghost ship. I was in the middle of my cycle, and I didn't have my diaphragm with me. It was a dumb, stupid thing to do."

"Why'd you wait so long to tell me?"

"I was hoping you'd want to keep it."

"That's all I need."

"I almost told you the day we got caught in the rain. In that old junk car. But I lost my nerve."

They sat there awhile in silence, looking at the moving figures on the screen.

"The first time I had my period I was afraid I was bleeding to death," she said. "I didn't know what it was. I told my mama and she took me into the bathroom and showed me the box of tampons, told me how to use them. But she didn't tell me about the risk you take when you let a man get close to you, the risk of ending up scared and alone with a little life growing inside of you."

"You're not alone," he said. The car seemed to be spinning around and around, as if it had been picked up by a twister.

"Right."

He put his hand on hers, but she moved it away.

"Sex is God's joke on the universe."

Zeb stared at the figures up on the screen. He could see their lips move, but couldn't hear their voices. This is what it's like to be deaf, he thought.

Later, on the way back to her house, Jenny said, "I don't have any money for an abortion."

"It's all right," he said. "I'll take care of it."

"What are friends for, right?"

Zeb stared at the white line in the center of the road. Jenny was blaming herself but wasn't he at fault, too? Why in the hell didn't he have the sense to use a rubber?

"Are you Zeb?" the nurse asked.

He looked up from the magazine. "Yes."

"Come on back."

He followed her through the door, down a hall. "Jenny O.K.?"

"Yes. She's in here. You can go in."

He stepped into the room. Jenny lay on a narrow bed, covered up with a sheet.

"Does it hurt?" he asked, taking her hand in his. Her hand was cool, damp.

"Only a little."

He looked around the room, at the sink, mirror, table, and chair. Her skirt, blouse, and panties were folded on the chair. On the table there was a box of tissues and a shiny silver instrument that resembled tongs.

"How do they do it?"

"With suction." She took a sharp breath, as if from a sudden pain. He tightened his grip on her hand.

A pockmarked man in a white lab coat came in. "Are you bleeding?"

"No," Jenny said. "This is Zeb, Dr. Gorman."

The doctor nodded at Zeb, then handed Jenny a sheet of paper. "Here are a list of things you should know. Any problems, like bleeding or heavy cramps, you should call the office. I want you to come back next week for a checkup."

Jenny nodded. She was still holding Zeb's hand.

"You can get dressed now." The doctor gave her a tight-lipped smile before he left.

"Charming guy," Zeb said.

"He's a gynecologist who specializes in infertility problems," Jenny said. "I don't think he does many of these." She sat up, pulling down the sheet. "Hand me my clothes, will you?"

The waiting room was full of pregnant women. Zeb paid the bill at the window, and he and Jenny went out to the parking lot.

"Do you want to come over for dinner tomorrow night?" She was still holding his hand. The sky was the color of ashes.

"I have to go to Seaton. My brother is getting married tomorrow."

Jenny's lower lip began trembling. He put his arm around her.

A sudden gust of wind showered them with yellow leaves.

Zeb, Merle, and L.C. stood at the altar in Gibbons Baptist, waiting for Theresa. The organist in the choir loft began playing the bridal theme, and everyone turned in their seats to watch Theresa make her entrance and glide down the aisle on her father's arm. She approached Merle, and they all turned and faced the preacher at the podium. "Dearly beloved..." he began. Soon Merle and Theresa joined hands, and, staring into each other's eyes, they took turns reciting from the Book of Ruth: *Entreat me not to leave thee: for whither thou goest, I will go, and where thou lodgest, I will lodge...*

Their hopefulness moved Zeb to tears. God have mercy on you both, he thought.

After the ceremony, he stood in the foyer as the guests hugged and congratulated the bride and groom. He hugged them, too, and kissed Theresa on her cheek.

He wandered away from the church, to the cemetery out back, and soon found himself standing in front of Lavis's tombstone. Someone, probably Mama, had put fresh flowers on the grave. He thought he might feel pity or sorrow or anger, but he was surprised to find he felt nothing at all. He was just acutely conscious of the clear, gold light, the chattering squirrels, the dry leaves rustling in the wind. He tried to pray but found himself thinking of a story he had read recently in the newspaper. A man had been arrested for killing a duck in a city park. He had held the duck by its feet and beat its brains out against a tree. Now why would somebody want to do that? Zeb wondered.

Jadine met him at the back door of the farmhouse, where the reception was being held.

"Now, Zeb, you be sure and say 'hey' to all my brothers and sisters. They've been asking about you."

He circulated among the guests, exchanging greetings with his aunts, uncles, and cousins. After Theresa introduced him to her parents, Zeb slipped outside and sat under the peach tree, watching a group of children playing in the back yard. The children joined hands and danced around the peach tree. A boy and girl stood inside the circle, passing a peach back and forth. Juice ran down their chins onto their clothes.

Overhead, a spider was busily spinning a web around a luna moth, wrapping it up in a cocoon. Zeb felt a sudden stab of horror when he realized the moth was only paralyzed. He wondered if it realized what was going on.

When he got back to Cedar Springs, he stopped by to see Jenny. She sat across from him at the kitchen table, her hands folded in front of her. "How was the wedding?"

"O.K."

"Did you kiss the bride?"

"Sure."

179

Jenny's lower lip trembled.

"This is hard for me to do," she said, "but I don't want to see you for a while."

"Why not?"

"I've been expecting too much from you, from this relationship. I know, it's my problem, not yours. But in order to deal with it, I'm going to have to stop seeing you."

"I don't understand."

"I got hurt real bad by a man a couple of years back. I thought we were in love, but it turned out he was lying to me and using me. I'm not accusing you of that—you've been honest and straight with me. But I don't want to get hurt again."

"I don't want you to get hurt, either."

"That's already happened. I had a hard and lonely winter last year. Then it was spring, and you were at my door. I thought, what the hell, I'll take a chance on this guy. I should have been more careful, shouldn't I?"

"I really care about you, Jenny. I—"

"Please—don't say any more."

"I'm sorry, Jenny."

"It's all right. I set myself up for it."

"I'd like to keep seeing you."

"Not now. I can't handle it."

Zeb felt as if there were suddenly less oxygen in the room, making it difficult for him to get his breath. He tried to think of something to say that would change her mind, but he could tell by the determined look in her eyes that nothing he could say would do any good. He closed his eyes and took several deep breaths. He could hear the wind chimes tinkling on the back porch.

"Guess I'll be going, then."

"Goodbye."

"Jenny—"

"*Goodbye*, Zeb."

He went out to his truck.

He drove down to the Saloon, where he began drinking down shots of whiskey, with beer as a chaser.

"I'm no good for her," he told Sloe Gin, after his seventh shot of whiskey, "and she knows it. I'm too scared."

"What are you scared of, Zeb?"

"Everything."

"How about another shot?"

"Good idea." Zeb drank the whiskey down quickly, chasing it with a swallow of beer. The barstool seemed to be rising and falling, like a ship on the sea. "I should have told her I loved her," he said. "I never even had the guts to tell her that."

"It's not too late to tell her," Sloe Gin said.

"Yes it is. She wants me to leave her alone now."

Zeb got up and went into the bathroom. The mirror was cracked, and his image was split in half. He moved around the john, looking at himself from different positions, but regardless of where he stood, his face was fractured by the broken glass.

"This Goddamn place is falling apart." His voice sounded like someone talking from the bottom of a well.

Duane woke him up the next morning, pounding on the door.

"I'm too sick to work today, Duane."

"I believe it. Look like you been wrestling with a troll."

"I'll be O.K. tomorrow."

"You need to lay off that booze."

After Duane left, Zeb stumbled back to the bathroom and fell on his knees in front of the toilet, vomiting a green, viscous fluid. He sat on the side of the bed, holding his aching head in his hands. He felt as if all his inner moorings had been eaten away. He felt as if he were in danger of flying apart, leaving pieces of himself sticking to the walls like silly putty.

What he needed was a cold beer.

In the refrigerator he found a partial loaf of bread, a can of dog food, a jar of mayonnaise, a pot of Jenny's homemade vegetable soup, and, on the bottom shelf, three cans of beer. The first beer made his headache go away; the second one banished his nausea.

He took a shower, put on clean clothes, and went outside to check the mailbox by the road. The sky was the color of concrete. He had the disturbing sense that the junk cars were watching him go by.

He found two letters in the mailbox, one from Jadine, the other from Willie Lee. He read his mother's letter first.

Dear Zeb,

L.C. came to see me a few nights ago and told me about that horrible massacre and about how he still dreams about the people who were killed. He asked me to forgive him for causing me so much worry. He put his head in my lap and cried. I know the Lord has his hand on him. ("He healeth the broken in heart and bindeth up their wounds.") He will meet us at the point of our greatest need, but first we have to ask Him for His help. L.C. and I prayed together, the way we used to do when you boys were little.

His trial is set for November 3rd. But I'm not as worried as I was. I can already feel some good coming from this, because it has helped L.C. get his pain and guilt out where he can face them. And it's also brought us closer together.

Merle and Theresa are off to their honeymoon in Jamaica. I'm so happy for them. I can't wait until they have a baby.

I hope to see you long before Christmas.

Love,
Mama

Next Zeb read the letter from Willie Lee.

Zeb, I just wanted to remind ya to be ready to go to Atlanta the 28th. Be at my house around nine AM. I know things have been a little slow this month, but I've got a feeling November is going to be a lot better.

Yours in the spirit of joy,

Willie Lee

Lying on his couch, Zeb stared up at Miss April 1956. She was leaning over a car's engine, wearing only skintight jeans and a mechanic's cap. The caption read, *Miss April can handle all your auto needs.* It occurred to him that he had no idea what time it was since he hadn't wound his clock in days. He got up and picked up the telephone, dialing the number for the time of day. A recorded voice said, "I'm sorry, but the time of day has been disconnected." He listened to the voice say this three more times before he hung up. He was starting to feel sick again.

Twenty-three

Zeb sat alone at the bar in the Saloon, drinking a whiskey sour. The Halloween crowd was starting to come in. Sloe Gin was an angel. Another bartender wore a helmet, a gas mask, and Army fatigues.

"Ye gods," Eli said, clapping Zeb on the back, "the scariest goblin I've seen tonight."

Eli was dressed as a monk, in a brown robe and sandals. Viv was with him. She wore a tunic covered with red and yellow patches that had been cut into the shapes of stars, lightning bolts, and quarter moons.

"They crucified a thief today," she said. "Some people claim he's the Messiah. They've laid his body to rest in a cave south of town. Tonight we're going to roll away the stone."

"His followers are expecting a miracle," Eli said. "Boy, are they going to be disappointed."

"Come with us, Zeb," said Viv.

"Not tonight."

"This man can't accompany us. He has no disguise, other than this pitiful mask of sorrow."

"That's not a mask," Viv said. "Can't you see he has a broken heart?"

Eli bowed. "My apologies, sir."

Zeb could see her walking on the beach, her hands full of seashells, and trying to play that out-of-tune guitar. And bathing last winter in her kitchen. While he had been in Atlanta, she was all he had been able to think about.

He paid for his whiskey and went to the pay phone by the front door. He dialed a number he had memorized but never used. "Listen, I have to see you tonight."

"Out of the question, Zeb," Roseanne said. "I'm going out."

"It's an emergency."

"I can't help it. I've got a date."

"How about afterwards? Just for a few minutes."

"Are you drunk?"

"No, I just want to talk to you."

"I can't believe you're doing this."

"I've left you alone until now, haven't I?"

Roseanne didn't answer.

"Just this once. Please."

"Do you know where I live?"

"Duplex on Emerson."

Roseanne was quiet so long he drifted off into a reverie of their last sweet days in New Orleans, before everything went to ruin.

"If you come by, make it after midnight," she finally said. "And only if I'm awake. Don't bother me if the lights are out. Do you hear me, Zeb?"

"Yes."

"I mean it about the lights. I won't answer the door if they're out. Do you understand?"

"I understand."

Roseanne was dressed as a cigarette girl. She wore a black miniskirt, a tray of cigarettes on a sling around her neck. Her date wore a black cape, a top hat, and carried a cane. Zeb sat in his truck, across from her apartment, and watched them walk up the walkway to her door. It was after one AM.

They turned to look when he closed the door of the truck.

"Oh, shit," Roseanne said. "Zeb, give me a couple of minutes, will you?"

He got back into the truck. Roseanne and her date were talking by the door. He pulled her against him and kissed her. Zeb looked away.

When he looked again, the man was walking to his car. Roseanne had gone into her apartment.

He crossed the street and knocked on the storm door. He could see her sitting on the couch. She motioned for him to come in.

He went in and sat in a chair across from her. Her mascara had run, leaving dark smudges around her eyes. She had taken off the tray of cigarettes.

"You just ruined a perfect evening."

He didn't say anything.

"What did you want to see me about?"

He got up and sat beside her. She smelled of sweat, cigarettes, beer. "Roseanne . . ."

"What in the hell is wrong with you?"

He put his face in his hands. What was he doing here, with this stranger? Some black Halloween magic had changed his love into a hard-eyed cigarette girl.

"Look at you," he said. "Why'd you have to change, huh?"

Jenny's house was dark and her car was gone. Her back door was unlocked. He went into the kitchen and turned on the light. On the table he found a pile of bills, some canceled checks and a sheet of paper—a projected budget of household expenses. He wondered where she was.

The cat was crying at the door. He let her in and gave her some milk. Then he went into Jenny's bedroom and lit the candle on the stand beside her bed. She had hung her painting of the lighthouse on the wall. He stood there awhile, staring at the painting. It was her effort to transmute her grief and rage at the loss of her father into the healing force of art. In a flash he could see how crippled he was, how estranged from his own natural forces. He had come back to Cedar Springs to try to pick up the broken pieces of his life and start over, but he hadn't been able to do it, and suddenly he could see why: he hadn't gone back far enough. To rebuild his life he was going to have to go back even farther, just like Jenny had done with the lighthouse. He had to go all the way back to the beginning—the place where everything had started going wrong.

He blew out the candle and went out to his truck.

As he drove down the road toward the junkyard, Zeb rolled down the window of the truck so he feel the cold night air on his skin. The wind singing in his ears, he composed a mental letter to Willie Lee: *I just wanted to let you know I have decided to give up on the future and concentrate on the past. It was a real experience playing with your band. Best of luck finding a new fiddler. Zeb*

Twenty-four

Zeb pulled into the Phillips 66 station and got out to stretch his muscles. To the left of the station was a concession stand displaying jugs of cider, country hams, bushel baskets full of potatoes, peanuts, apples. Leather whips and Confederate flags hung from the rafters. Next to the stand there was a steel cage with a black bear inside.

The attendant wore a denim jacket and a cowboy hat with a snakeskin band. "How much, hoss?"

"Fill it up." Zeb walked over to look at the bear, which looked to be about half grown. It lay among its own turds while two teenage boys jabbed at it with sticks. One of the sticks hit the bear in the eye. It grunted and moved to another corner, lying down in more excrement.

Zeb went back to pay for the gas. "Who owns the bear?"

"Me. I own this whole place."

"Bear like that ought to be out in the woods, eating blackberries."

"Whose bear is he—yours or mine?"

"He's yours, I guess. But how would you like to be locked up in a cage with your own shit?"

The man pulled back his jacket, showing Zeb a holstered revolver on his belt. "You pass this way again, keep going. I don't want your business."

Zeb drove out of the station thinking he'd be back, anyway.

He was on Route 12, near the Alsace Highway, about five miles from Lavis's homeplace. A few miles farther down the highway he turned into the long driveway leading back to Huis Yardley's mansion. Massive oaks lined the driveway, their leaves the color of gold coins. He parked behind a Cadillac limousine and walked up the steps to the porch, staring up at the white columns. He lifted the brass knocker and let it fall twice.

An elderly black man wearing a white shirt and tie answered the door.

"Can I help you, sir?"

"I'd like to see Mr. Yardley."

"What is the nature of your business with Mr. Yardley?"

"I'd like to talk to him about some property he owns."

"Your name, sir?"

"Zeb Dupree."

"Wait here, please."

Zeb tried to recall the few times he had seen Amos Yardley, Sumner County's richest resident, a man Lavis had said could buy everything Rainy owned with his spare cash. Zeb had seen Mr. Yardley riding down Main Street in the back of his chauffeured limousine a few times, and back in high school he had seen him coming out of a lawyer's office on Main Street. Mr. Yardley had been old even then.

When the ancient butler returned he said, "Mr. Yardley will see you now."

Zeb stepped into a hallway and looked up at a chandelier suspended from the ceiling.

"This way, please."

He followed the old man down a hallway, past the stairs, and through several large, cool rooms to a smaller room at the rear of the mansion, full of windows, where Mr. Yardley sat in a rocking chair beneath an oil painting of Robert E. Lee. Mr. Yardley wore a purple robe over white pajamas. His face was as wrinkled as a peach pit. Only a few tufts of hair remained on his mottled skull.

"Mr. Yardley, my name is Zeb Dupree," Zeb said, shaking the old man's bony hand. "I went to Cedar Springs State with your grandson, Huis."

"Huis? You know Huis?"

"Yes, sir. How's he doing now?"

"Doing right well, I should say. He's a lawyer up in Greensboro. Married a little gal who's richer than six foot up a bull's ass. Family owns a string of cotton mills. You want some iced tea?"

"Yes, sir."

Mr. Yardley picked up a cowbell from a stand beside his rocker and gave it a shake. "Now, what's the purpose of your visit?"

"I'm interested in buying an old house you own down on the river, along with a few acres of land."

"I got a lot of old houses. Which one you referring to?"

"This one used to belong to Elkins Dupree."

"Elkins bought that farm from Thaddeus Brett, back before the first World War. He came down here from Virginia, married into the Crawford family. Most of the white Crawfords have died or moved away now. There's still plenty of colored Crawfords around, though."

A coffee-colored woman wearing a white uniform appeared. Mr. Yardley asked her to bring a pitcher of tea, then went on talking.

"You're too young to remember Clem Crawford. He went mad after he caught a disease from a whore up in Richmond. Claimed he could hear rabbits and trees talking to him. Clem got to running around Seaton in his drawers, chasing butterflies and talking to trees. His family had to tie him to his bed. Kept him tied up till the day he died."

"Imagine that," Zeb said.

"Folks said it was the wrath of God coming down on Clem for consorting with a whore, but I always figured the Lord had bigger things to worry about than Clem's sex life. Plain truth of the matter was Clem Crawford always was unlucky, and he should have had enough sense to wear a rubber."

The woman returned with a tray containing a pitcher of tea and two tall glasses of ice.

"Now why are you interested in the Dupree place?"

"Elkins was my grandfather."

"I'll tell you something about Elkins." Mr. Yardley placed his hand near his knee. "He had a dick down to here. You ain't built like that, are you?"

"No, sir," Zeb said, embarrassed by the presence of the woman.

"So it don't run in the family?"

"Not as far as I'm concerned."

"Well, that's good to hear. Fellow built like that can wreck some homes if he gets to running around the countryside."

Mr. Yardley took a drink of tea. "What were you planning to do with the place?"

"I'd like to fix it up and live in it."

"Take right much fixing to get that house into any kind of decent condition."

"I realize that, sir."

"How much land you interested in acquiring?"

"Maybe ten acres."

"That's some mighty good land on the river. People call me all the time about that land, wanting to buy it."

"What does it usually bring per acre?"

"I don't know, son. I don't sell land very often. Mostly I buy it."

"My daddy loved that place. He used to talk about it all the time. Used to drive me out there and talk about growing up there."

"Your daddy the one that shot himself?"

"Yes, sir."

"Where do you live?"

"Cedar Springs."

"You planning to come back here?"

"If I can buy that place, I am."

"Well, let me think on it. Come on back and see me in a couple of days."

Zeb spent a few minutes listening to the old man brag about Huis, how smart he was to have gotten himself married to a rich woman. Then he said he guessed he'd be going. Mr. Yardley rang the cowbell again, and the old butler appeared.

"How does he know the ring is for him?" Zeb asked.

"We got a little signal worked out."

After Zeb left he drove down to the old man's homeplace and stood in the dank front room, trying to visualize the place restored: rotting boards and beams replaced, new windows and doors, the floors sanded and polished, a new roof, coats of paint inside and out, the yard landscaped. A mouse ran along a mattress in the corner, disappearing into a hole in the wall. The room stunk of urine and wine. Suddenly, Zeb felt overwhelmed by the task before him. He climbed the stairs and stood in one of the front rooms, looking out at the river, gray as wood smoke in the autumn haze. This had been Lavis's room, where he used to lie in bed at night as a boy. He thought about the way his father's life had been irrevocably changed by the loss of his homeplace, and how, after-wards, he had just flopped around like a fish on the river bank, in bitter bondage to Rainy, unable to rise above his loss. I've been going down the same way, he thought. But now I've got to set things right.

Downstairs, in the kitchen, he saw a commode in the center of the floor. A table lay on its side in one corner, beside an empty Wild Irish Rose bottle. Cans, bottles, bits of broken glass, and playing cards were scattered about. There was a moldy boot in the sink.

He went through the back door, down the steps, through the weeds to the barn, where Elkins had once had his blacksmith's shop. In the dim light he saw a rusted Ford truck from the 1940's. A barn owl stared down at him from the rafters.

"You'd better get used to me," Zeb said. "I'm going to be around for a while."

When he went back to see Mr. Yardley, the old man said he'd take twenty-three thousand dollars for the house plus ten acres.

"Is there oil on that land?" Zeb asked.

"There's liable to be."

"I can give you sixteen thousand."

"Look here, Dupree, you want me to just *give* you the land?"

"No, sir. I just don't believe I can raise twenty-three thousand."

"That's about what the place is worth, way I figure it. Course, it would be worth more if there was oil on it."

"I was just joking about the oil."

"Well now, there could be oil on that land. There just could be. And how do you think I'd feel if you discovered oil on land I'd sold you at such a bargain? Tell you how I'd feel—like a fool."

"You're welcome to keep the oil rights," Zeb said, wishing he'd kept his mouth shut.

"I should hope so."

"I might be able to raise eighteen thousand."

"You wouldn't come in here and try to take advantage of a sick old man, now would you?"

"No, sir. It's just that twenty-three thousand is a lot of money for ten acres and a house that's falling down."

Mr. Yardley snorted, but Zeb could tell he was enjoying himself immensely—the shrewd old fart. "You could tear the house down."

"I want to fix it up, the way it was when my daddy was a boy."

Mr. Yardley took a drink of tea. When he set the glass down, tea ran down his chin onto his pajamas. "I might be able to let it go for twenty-one thousand, seeing as how you know Huis. But that's the absolute best I can do."

"I'll need a little time to see about getting the money. Can I come back tomorrow?"

"I'll be here if the good Lord lets me live," the old man said.

It was time to go see L.C.

Zeb still had about four thousand dollars left in savings from his share of the settlement with Roseanne. He could use that to begin renovating the house. He would have to get L.C. to cosign a bank loan for the house and land. L.C. was certainly in good financial condition. Not only did he own his own house free and clear, but he also had a good income, a couple of savings accounts, and a half interest in a thriving wrecker business. L.C. was currently in the county jail in Riverville, serving a forty-five-day sentence for shooting up the Confederate statue. Still, everyone agreed that the judge had gone easy on him, largely due to the efforts of L.C.'s attorney, who had built his defense around the trauma his client had experienced in Vietnam. The lawyer called a psychiatrist to the stand, who dazzled everyone with phrases like "compulsive flashback disorder" and "post-traumatic stress syndrome." In addition to the jail term, the judge also fined L.C. a thousand dollars, put him on two years' probation, and ordered him to pay for restoring the statue.

Zeb drove to Riverville and parked behind the jail across from the courthouse. He went into the jail and asked to see L.C. The jailer escorted L.C. out to the visitors' room.

Zeb talked to his brother a few minutes before he got around to asking him to cosign for the bank loan to buy the old man's homeplace.

"You were trying to burn that house down a couple of months ago," L.C. said.

"That was then."

"It would take a fortune to fix that place up."

"I know it will take a lot of work, L.C., but I want to do it."

"I'm laying back there staring at the bars, and the man comes back to tell me my brother's here to see me. This causes me to feel a warm glow. I tell myself, 'L.C., you ain't been forgotten by your blood kin down here in the jailhouse. Your brother has come all the way down from Cedar Springs to see you.' About a damned bank loan."

"That place should be back in the family."

"Back in the family, huh?"

"You going to help me?"

L.C. looked at Zeb awhile before he spoke.

"Yeah. But I think you're crazy as a shithouse bat."

Twenty-five

Zeb was in the front yard of Lavis' homeplace, cutting down weeds with a sling blade. He heard Henry barking and turned around to see a heavyset black man standing in the road.

"That dog bite?"

"Not usually. Hush, Henry."

The man stepped into the yard, keeping an eye on Henry, who was sniffing his leg. He wore jeans, a flannel shirt and a slouch hat. A medium brown color, he looked to be in his early forties. "You must be the fellow buying this place."

"That's right?"

"Going to tear that old house down?"

"No, I'm planning to restore it."

"Got yourself a job there."

"I've got time," Zeb said, giving the weeds another whack with the blade.

"This house used to belong to a Dupree."

"That was my grandfather."

"Elkins Dupree was married to a Crawford. My mother is a Crawford."

"That right?" Zeb eyed the remaining weeds he had to cut.

"She's kin to the Crawfords used to live on this road, onliest they never claimed her being as she's black and they white." Jake took a plug of tobacco from his pocket and bit off a chew.

"How is she kin?"

"Jacob Crawford was the granddaddy of Ruth Crawford, who was married to Elkins Dupree. Jacob had a slave named Isabelle. She had a son by Jacob, named Benjamin. He was my mama's granddaddy. It's all wrote down in the Bible we got from my great grandmama if you ever care to see it."

They were both quiet awhile, Zeb hitting at the weeds, Jake working on the tobacco.

"Small world, ain't it?" Zeb said.

Jake was squatting now, petting Henry.

"What happened to his eye?"

"He got it put out."

Later, when Zeb drove out to the highway, he saw Jake sitting on the porch of his two-story frame house, along with a white man in a wheelchair. Clothes hanging on a line in the back yard undulated in the breeze.

Jake and Zeb waved at exactly the same time.

In the attic of the old house, in the bottom of a cedar chest, he found a mildewed scrapbook that had belonged to his grandmother. The scrapbook contained some grainy, yellow photographs of his grandparents and Lavis and Ganton when they were boys; letters to Zeb's grandmother, most of them from her sister in Raleigh; and newspaper clippings about births, deaths, and marriages of distant relatives in Virginia and the Carolinas. In one photo Lavis and Ganton had their arms around each other's shoulders. In another, Lavis was just a baby, and his mother was holding him in her arms. Beside her stood Elkins, stiff and poker-faced, in a dark suit.

Zeb took the scrapbook home and showed it to Jadine.

"I thought Lavis had gotten everything out of that house long ago. I guess he missed that."

They sat on the couch in the den, looking through the scrapbook.

"Lavis's parents were hardworking, God-fearing people, who expected a lot from their sons," Jadine said. "I believe he always felt bad because he didn't think he'd lived up to their expectations."

"What did it matter after they were dead?"

"The dead go on living in their children, Zeb. That's one reason why being a parent is such a big responsibility."

Zeb was looking at a photo of Lavis and Elkins. "I talked to the loan officer at the bank. The loan went through O.K. I should close on the house and land next week."

"If you really want that old house, that's your business. But you know you could take the same amount of money and buy a nice little house in town, like L.C. And you could build a brand new house for what it's going to cost to restore that one."

"I know that, Mama."

Jadine closed the scrapbook and looked steadily at him. "You're doing it for him, aren't you?"

"Not really. I just hate to see the place go down."

Driving down to the house, he saw Jake standing by his mailbox, and he stopped to say hello.

"How's work on the house coming?" Jake asked.

"I've got the trash and junk cleaned out. I'm prying up the rotten boards now."

"Spect you're finding a lot of those."

"Right many. But the floor's solid in most places."

"That's something to be thankful for. Care for a cup of coffee?"

"Sure." Zeb parked the truck and went with Jake up to the porch.

"How do you like yours?"

"Black."

"Have a seat. I'll be right back."

Zeb sat in one of two chairs to the left of the door and watched Henry sniffing around in the yard. He wondered what kin he was to Jake since they both had the same great-great-grandfather. He thought they might be cousins of some sort, but he wasn't sure. He would have to ask Jadine.

Jake returned with two mugs of steaming coffee. He handed one to Zeb and sat down in the porch swing. "I have to go back to work tonight. Been off two days."

"Where do you work?"

"Hospital. I'm an orderly on the night shift."

The door opened and a plump, dark-skinned woman came out, pulling a wheelchair after her. Seated in the wheelchair was a slender white man who looked to be in his late thirties. He wore a neatly pressed white shirt, khaki trousers, and a blue windbreaker.

"Hello," Zeb said, standing up.

"Morning," said the woman. "You can sit down."

"This is Mr. Zeb Dupree, young man who's buying the old house down the road. This is my wife, Olivia."

"Nice to meet you, Mr. Dupree." Olivia sat down in the chair next to Zeb. The man in the wheelchair was staring at the road.

"Please call me Zeb."

"That was a fine house in its day," Olivia said. "Be nice to see it fixed up again."

"It's going to take a lot of work."

"Most things do." Olivia smoothed down a section of the white man's thinning hair with her hand.

"That there is Claude," Jake said. "I ain't introduced you all because he ain't right. Used to be a professor before he ruint hisself."

"How'd he do that?"

"Shot hisself in the head."

"Why?"

"On account of his wife. She run off with another man. And the blues come floating down into his heart like a black buzzard."

"We keep Claude for his mama and daddy," Olivia said. "They don't want to put him in a nursing home. Too expensive."

"Olivia is a registered nurse," Jake said proudly.

"How you doing today, Claude?" Zeb asked.

"You wasting your time talking to him," Jake said. "Claude is done gone over the rainbow."

"Claude was real smart before he got hurt. He was a history professor at Duke University."

"His parents ever come to see him?"

Olivia shook her head. "They just send a check every month."

"His wife come to see him once. She was mighty fine-looking, but I ain't never seen a woman I'd shoot myself over."

"She only stayed a few minutes. She never came back."

"He ever get any birthday cards or letters?"

"They wouldn't have no meaning for him," Jake said.

"The first year we kept him I made him a cake on his birthday," Olivia said. "He just sat there and stared at it. Jake had to blow out the candles."

"He ever say anything?"

"Not a word." Jake leaned forward and pointed to a star-shaped scar on Claude's right temple. "That's where the bullet went in. His hair is growing over the place where it came out, so you can't see it so good."

"Why don't you let me take Claude down to the farm? He can keep me company while I work."

"Be fine with me," Jake said, "long as Olivia don't mind."

"I don't mind. Fresh air would be good for him."

When he finished his coffee, Zeb said he guessed he would be going. Jake picked Claude up and carried him down to the truck. Zeb opened the door so Jake could set him down in the seat. Olivia pushed the wheelchair out to the truck, and Zeb put it in the back next to the door he had bought at Seaton Building Supply. "Come on, Henry." Henry jumped into the truck bed, and Zeb shut the gate.

"I don't think he'll mess in his britches," Olivia said. "He's already done that this morning. If he does, you can bring him on back and I'll change him."

On the way to Lavis's homeplace, Claude stared straight ahead, his thin hands folded in his lap. Zeb parked in the yard and got the wheelchair out of the back of the truck, pushing it around to the passenger side of the truck. Opening the door he picked Claude up and set him down in the wheelchair. Claude smelled like soap and baby powder. Zeb pushed the wheelchair through the yard to the front porch steps. "You can sit here and keep me company while I work." He went back to the truck for the door, carrying it on his shoulders up to the porch. He returned to the truck for his tools and the bag of hinges and screws for the door. When he passed Claude again, he said, "That's a nice breeze off the river today."

Claude was staring down at his hands.

Zeb put the hinges on the new door; then he picked it up and set it down in the door jamb. He attached the hinges to the frame, then stepped back, opening and closing the door. He would need to adjust it with a carpenter's level next time he came out. "No use to lock it now," he said, fitting the key in the lock. "Someone could just go in through a window."

He sat down on the porch steps and looked at Claude.

"My daddy grew up here," he said, "back during a time when there were panthers in the woods, and a big bear named Sam Crockett that lived back in Wildcat Swamp . . ."

At night Zeb lay in bed, his arms and shoulders sore, blisters on his hands, his mind racing over different sections of the house and land, which he had already begun to commit to memory. He would need to climb up on the roof and nail some plastic over the hole to keep out the rain; the window sills would need to be replaced before he could install new windows; he would have to replace the floor over the living room and the beams that supported the porch roof. He could get Merle and L.C. to help with that. He would have to pull down the ivy and honeysuckle and buy new appliances and fixtures. Then there was all the sanding and painting that needed to be done. He could ask Duane to come down from Cedar Springs and give him a price on the entire job. Since about half the land he was buying was cleared, he could plant a garden in the spring and sell vegetables out of it, along with apples from the orchard behind the barn. But that was a long-term project; in the meantime he would need to do something else to meet his bank payments and raise money for renovations. He would also need money to live.

Although he once would have thought the idea ludicrous, he now had no problem going to *The Seaton Gazette* to talk to the editor, Shelby James, about a job. Shelby, a plump, ruddy-faced man in his late fifties, had been editor of the paper ever since Zeb could remember. Shelby seemed impressed with Zeb's credentials, his education, writing awards, and clips, and he was sympathetic regarding Zeb's explanation for losing his job in New Orleans. Zeb blamed the loss on his marriage breakup. He didn't mention Lavis.

"I'm on my third marriage myself, Zeb, and I've learned the hard way that a woman brings a man into the world, and she sure as hell can take him on out, too."

Shelby said he had a part-time reporter's position opening soon. "Now it wouldn't pay a lot, just a hundred and fifty a week, but it could work into a full-time position by, say, next spring."

"I'd sure like to have the job, but do you think you could pay a little more than that?" Zeb was thinking of the money he needed to fix up the house.

Shelby said he would see what he could do.

Every morning Zeb took Claude down to the farmhouse and talked to him while he worked. He would tell Claude first one thing and then another—how Oscar's cancer had gone into remission, gossip his mother told him at night from Finley's, plans he had for fixing up the house, and how he had felt when he closed on the homeplace ("like I was dreaming"). He told Claude he knew how he felt about losing his wife, because he had lost his wife, too, and although at the time it had felt like the end of the world, he could see now that it was for the best. "She represented perfection for me, Claude, but I don't think you can find that in this world." He told Claude about Lavis, his bitterness at losing the homeplace, and how he was making things right by buying it and fixing it up. And he told him about his former girlfriend, Jenny O'Brian, whom he couldn't seem to stop thinking about. "She's a fine woman with a pure heart, but I didn't have the good sense or the nerve to claim her."

At first Claude paid him no attention at all, but the more Zeb talked, the more he began to feel that the man was actually listening. Claude would watch him while he talked, especially when he didn't think Zeb was looking at him.

Each day around noon Zeb would take a break and feed Claude the lunch that Olivia had sent along in a paper bag. She usually sent a mixture of pureed chicken and vegetables in a bowl, along with crackers and a soft drink. Zeb would talk to Claude while he ate; afterwards, he would wipe the remaining food from Claude's mouth and face with a napkin, and lift the can to his mouth so he could drink.

Claude's skin was surprisingly smooth and delicate for a man his age. His eyes, like an infant's, were a soft shade of blue.

One afternoon when he was taking a break from working on the house, Zeb got out his notepad and pen and wrote Jenny a letter:

Dear Jenny,

I am living in Seaton and trying to fix up my daddy's home-place on the Choctoosie River. I bought the house plus ten acres, and I'm planning on raising some vegetables on the land to help pay the mortgage. It's slow going, but it's going to be worth it when I get it all restored. I'd like for you to come down and see it some-time. Truth is, I'd just like to see you, because I've been thinking about you a lot and missing you. I don't blame you for breaking up with me. I had a lot of things to work out, and I think that prevented me from being the kind of man you needed. But I'm getting my life together now, and I hope you'll give me another chance someday. Even if you don't I want you to know I love you. Zeb

He read the letter over, and then folded it up and put it in his pocket. He wasn't sure what she would think about the letter, or even if she would answer it. But at least he wanted to let her know how he felt.

One crisp morning in December, Zeb drove by the Phillips 66 station with the caged bear. He turned in and drove by the pumps, looking for the owner. A chunky boy came out of the station, one of the kids who had been jabbing the bear.

"Where's the boss?"

"Uncle Roy? He's gone to town. Can I help you with some-thing?"

"I just stopped by to look at the bear."

"That bag of bones brings in right smart amount of business."

The bear was lying in straw, pieces of shit clinging to its fur. It eyed him warily when he opened the gate and stepped into the cage.

"Get out of here," he said, waving his hat. "Move!"

He drove the bear out of the cage and around the back of the building. He watched it lumber into a clump of pines.

Coming back around the corner of the building, he bumped into the owner's nephew, who had a rifle. Zeb wrestled the gun away from him, and the boy dropped to his knees. "Don't shoot, mister! That's a thirty-ought-six."

"Tell your uncle something for me."

"Yes, sir. What do you want me to tell him?"

"Tell him he's a miserable asshole, and if I ever hear of him mistreating another animal, I'm coming back for him."

Zeb threw the rifle up on the roof.

Later that morning, after he and Claude had eaten lunch, he got out his fiddle and played "Arkansas Traveler" for Claude on the porch. Zeb wanted his music to flow over his friend like a healing stream, but Claude watched with the same detached expression he viewed everything else. Zeb closed his eyes and imagined a cliff, a body of water below: his childhood, which stared up at him with its lonesome blue eye of mercy. A three-quarter moon hung in the sky, the air smelled of ripe and rotting peaches. He could see Lavis and Rainy sitting in Rainy's truck, drinking whiskey from Dixie cups while Rainy dreamed of catfish ponds, watermelon and blueberry bonanzas, tobacco money floating down like leaves from the sky. He could see Lavis carrying him through the whispering corn and hear the old man's voice, telling him of his loss. He began playing "Soldier's Joy," Lavis's favorite song. The bow felt light as a fairy's wing in his fingers. The music flowed through his body, down into the porch of the old house, around and through the boards, up the walls and into the beams and slats, resonating in the rooms.

When he finished the tune, he asked, "What did you think of that, Claude?"

Claude was staring at a wren that had landed on the porch railing. He looked at Zeb, at the bird, and back at Zeb again.

Claude was opening and closing his mouth.

"What is it, Claude?" Zeb stood up and bent over him. "What is it?"

"Birrrrrrd," said Claude. "Birrrrrrrrrrrrrrd!"